RUNAWAY TO TAHITI

RUNAWAY TO TAHITI

▼

Harry F. McIntyre

Dear Pat,

I hope you enjoy the voyage of Rodger and Helen aboard the Sea Witch.

Harry McIntyre

iUniverse, Inc.
New York Lincoln Shanghai

RUNAWAY TO TAHITI

Copyright © 2006 by Harry F. McIntyre

All rights reserved. No part of this book may be used or reproduced by any means, graphic, electronic, or mechanical, including photocopying, recording, taping or by any information storage retrieval system without the written permission of the publisher except in the case of brief quotations embodied in critical articles and reviews.

iUniverse books may be ordered through booksellers or by contacting:

iUniverse
2021 Pine Lake Road, Suite 100
Lincoln, NE 68512
www.iuniverse.com
1-800-Authors (1-800-288-4677)

ISBN-13: 978-0-595-38488-4 (pbk)
ISBN-13: 978-0-595-82869-2 (ebk)
ISBN-10: 0-595-38488-9 (pbk)
ISBN-10: 0-595-82869-8 (ebk)

Printed in the United States of America

ACKNOWLEDGEMENTS

My everlasting gratitude to the members of four writing groups, of which I am a part, for their support and encouragement: The Seahurst Writers, The Timekeepers, The Lake Klahanee Writers, and the Highline Community College Writers.

Very special thanks to:

my wife, Selma, for her support and encouragement; Patrick Lettenmaier, Robert Hugh Ross, Ethyl Winters, Lona Jennings, and Denise Yanega for their critiquing expertise; Jeffery and Sean McGuire for their computer assistance; my publishing consultant, Michael Altman for helping me through the process of publishing, and last but not least, Rodger and Helen for allowing me to tag along behind them, take notes, and then write about it.

* * * *

T

Chapter 1

▼

½ Lead

A taxi wheeled past the entrance sign to the Des Moines, Washington marina, and screeched to a stop. Helen jumped out, leaned down to pay the driver, then hoisted a bulging sea bag across her shoulders, and headed toward the dock. Even at middle-age, she had a spring to her step; a body language that shouted "I'm in charge."

At the end of the dock, a Tahiti Ketch," Sea Witch" painted across her transom, bobbed gently in her moorage slip, and beside her, a still handsome, but gaunt, middle-aged man waits. His seaman-type clothes fit poorly, still having that "new look." His gray, loose-hanging turtleneck shirt makes him appear even thinner. Sailor dungarees, needing to be washed a few times to shrink and lose their still shiny look; a Greek fisherman's cap, not having developed proper crush and the lack of a sweat-line at the brow of the cap, complete the faux-seaman image. A well-used briar pipe hung loosely from his mouth as he watched the woman's descent down the gangway, the woman who sold him the ketch, the woman who will be his skipper for the trip to Tahiti.

Rodger had been at the dock for over an hour, arriving early on purpose. He wanted time alone with the "Sea Witch"; time to get acquainted with his new boat before setting out on what would be his last adventure. Once more, Rodger let his gaze slide over the thirty-foot ketch, its white hull and cabin, trimmed in navy blue at the waterline. He lifted his eyes toward the two masts with their attached booms rising above the deck, stained mahogany and set off by crisp, white sails flaked on their booms. The hardware, all in good repair, and all lines nearly new. *A classic boat built by a real craftsman. She's obviously been well maintained with probably a lot of nautical miles left in her.*

It all began when Rodger saw the Tahiti Ketch for sale in the Seattle Times. Maybe it had something to do with the fact he had just come from his doctor's office where he'd been told the tuberculosis was getting no better. He had a limited time to live, a limited time to do all the things he had wanted to do with his life. The ad with its reference to Tahiti brought the painful reminder he never would realize his life-long dream of sailing to Tahiti. But why not, he asked himself? This just might be a boat he could single-hand. He responded to the advertisement.

At their meeting, Rodger had been surprised to discover the boat's owner was a woman; one obviously quite knowledgeable about boats and sailing. It didn't take long for them to realize, Rodger was not. "I don't think you have the experience needed to pull this off," she'd cautioned once he'd confided his plan to her. "I'm afraid you couldn't handle this craft by yourself. It's not a single-hander for an amateur."

Rodger's disappointment had been keen, but he accepted that she was right. He had turned to leave when she stopped him. "Look, buy the boat from me, and I'll throw my skipper services in free. I've always wanted to take this trip."

"I may not survive to the journey's end," Rodger reminded her.

"So what?" She'd passed it off with a wave of her hand. "That we're going to die is a given; how and when is the unknown. My late husband, Clyde, used to say, 'Death is the sugar of life. It makes each day we live that much sweeter.' So, let's just do it." The determined set of her jaw told Rodger the decision had already been made as far as she was concerned.

* * * *

He watched the woman approach, a woman he scarcely knew. A small twinge of misgiving stirred inside him. *If only my family understood,* he thought. *If only they could have been down here to wish me Bon Voyage.* A nervous attempt to light his pipe sent him into a spasm of coughing. He leaned against the starboard gunnels of the boat until the coughing subsided. The doctor had said to get plenty of fresh air. *If fresh air is what it will take, I'll certainly get my share in the next few months.*

"I see you beat me here," the woman said as she paused beside the ketch, and then slung her seabag aboard. "Ready for the big adventure, Rodger?"

Rodger glanced across the bay; its water slightly ruffled by a gentle breeze, a summer sky laced with marestail-like clouds. Morning temperatures were in the sixties. *A great day to start our voyage,* he thought. "I'm as ready as I'll ever be."

Helen instructed Rodger to go below and start the small diesel engine. It would get them out of the marina and into the shipping lanes where current and wind would launch them on the first leg of their journey.

Rodger responded dutifully and soon returned, the engine idling smoothly. He then uncleated the bow and stern line, pushed off from the dock, and the Sea Witch was free to do what she was made for, to sail.

"In these light winds today we'll use the mainsail and the engine until we get to Point-No-Point. Then we'll douse the engine when we pick up stronger winds at the tip of the Kitsap Peninsula. As the wind freshens we can add the jib and mizzen sail. August is the best month for these waters, and crossing the Pacific Ocean should be a great adventure. By the way, can I call you Rod or Rodg instead of Rodger? Rodger sounds so formal," asked Helen as she stood at the tiller looking down at Rodger seated near her in the cockpit.

"Sure, just call me Rodg. Most everyone does. Is there anything that I should be doing Skipper? I want to pull my weight and be a good first mate." Rodger stood, ready to follow orders.

"Well, you could make the skipper a cup of coffee. There will be plenty to do later on, believe me," she warned.

Rodger went below to the small galley and lit the gimbaled, oil-burning cook stove. By the time the coffee was ready the cabin was a toasty warm and had begun to feel like a place two compatible people could share the sleeping, eating, cooking, and lounging all basically in the same space.

Rodger carried the two mugs of steaming coffee up the five-step stairway to the cockpit only to find Helen lost in a reverie. He stopped short and studied her for a moment. *She's attractive; at her age the auburn hair is probably tinted, but it sets off her green eyes well. Her ruddy complexion gives her a bit of an Irish look.* "It looks like you're lost in thought," Rodger ventured.

"Well, yes." Helen's cheeks flushed, "I...I was here on the Sea Witch, but Clyde was at the helm."

"Oh," offered Rodger gently. "That's easy enough to understand, Helen. I hope this trip will be all right for you."

"It will be, I just need a few days under my belt to get past the what-ifs. By the way, Rodg, you can bend on the jib and hoist it. The wind's picked up earlier than expected. Then we can shut the engine down and raise the mizzen sail."

"I can shut the engine down, but how do you bend on a jib?" asked Rodger as he carefully handed Helen her coffee.

Helen laughed, "I keep forgetting you're new at this. Take the tiller and my coffee cup and I'll show you how to bend on a jib." Helen hands her cup to Rodger, "Hold the course at 320 degrees while I take the sail out of the bag and fasten the metal fasteners located on the forward edge of the sail to the forestay. Attach that line, called a halyard, to the top of the sail and run it up to the top of the mast and cleat it off." She stepped back, hands on her hips, "That's called bending on the jib. We'll do the same with the main sail and the mizzen sail."

She retrieved her cup from Rodger before taking over the helm again. "Notice the sails are luffing or in shore lingo flapping. We're headed directly into the wind, so I'll fall off the heading about 15 degrees. Now, take the lines connected at the bottom corner of the jib, main, and mizzen sail and run them right-hand around the wenches located on the gunnels." Rodger took the lines, following Helen's instructions. "Tighten them and see what happens."

"Ah Ha! The sails fill with air and stop flapping or should I say luffing?"

"Notice the boat has picked up speed as the sails start to draw air."

"Wow!" Rodger could feel the boat surging forward, like a gazelle. With the sudden silence of the engine shut down, he could now hear the lapping sound of waves on the hull, and the sound of wind in the rigging. "This is so great."

"I agree," said Helen as she stood self confidently at the helm. "Now that the sails are up, let's do something about lunch."

"Give me your cup, Skipper, I'll go below and prepare it." As Rodger took out the ingredients to make sandwiches, a spasm of coughing overcame him. He sank weakly onto the nearby sleeping divan to regain his composure. As he quieted himself, his thoughts reverted to happenings preceding the trip. A twinge of doubt took foremost position in his thinking. *How sound was his decision to run off without any more explanation than the one page letter he left his wife, Irene. I tried to explain my need to fulfill this dream. I told her I'd call from my first port-of-call, to answer any questions she might have. There surely will be some questions, this has been my big secret, but I didn't want to give her the chance to talk me out of it.*

Ours wasn't an ideal marriage. Oh, I always well provided for her and our three sons, but the boys are adults now seeking their own pathway through life. There are the seven grandchildren who will fill some of Irene's time and probably satisfy her need for family. She's been running our mortgage company quite nicely since my health problem. Our oldest son, Junior, has stepped into my job, so all in all, everyone seems to get along without me very well...almost too well. Of course they'll grieve when I give in to the tuberculosis. But I need this adventure! It may shorten my life, but so what? It's not like I'm making the trip alone. I wonder why I was reluctant to mention in my letter the Skipper is a woman?

This fact brought him back to the moment. He finished the two sandwiches adding some chips and a couple of bottles of Old English 800 beer to the tray. Climbing the five steps to the cockpit, he placed the tray within Helen's reach. "I hope this meets your expectations, Captain."

"This looks good, Mate. Take the tiller after you open your beer, I'll just freshen up a bit before I dive in. I am hungry, must be all this fresh air. We should be on a heading of 290 degrees, stay as close to that as the wind allows. If the sails starts luffing, just fall off the wind a little until the sail fills again; just keep us off the beach. We must sail off the direction of the wind by at least 15 degrees to fill the sail and keep them from luffing. You'll get the hang of it pretty soon," Helen added with a grin before disappearing down the hatchway.

Rodger sat at the back of the cockpit with the tiller in his left hand, a beer in his right. He surveyed the shoreline and marveled at the beauty of Bainbridge Island and the Kitsap Peninsula as they sailed north at a hull speed of six knots. The waves were about a foot high created by the 10-knot wind coming directly out of the north. With a 290-degree setting Rodger guessed they were actually running 30 degrees off the wind direction. The boat was lying over noticeably and picking up speed. He felt the boat's response to the tiller and a moment's apprehension, as if he had a living cat-like animal by the tail.

This sailing is far different from any of my previous boating experiences, he mused. *This is a pulsing, surging, dynamic thing in rhythm with the water and the wind. Sailing is so wonderfully different from power boating.*

Helen appeared in the stairwell to the cabin. "Well Mate, how do you like sailing on a day with good wind, lots of sunshine and the temperature at 70 degrees?"

"Where has this been all my life? I just love it!"

"Good, because you're in for a whole lot of it before we get to Tahiti." Sitting down beside Rodger, she turned her attention to her lunch. "The sandwich is excellent, I'm glad you know your way around a galley. I can take or leave kitchen work. We'll trade off of course, but it's nice to know there are some decent meals in store when I'm not doing the cooking." She took a swallow of her beer. "I assume you were able to get the list of supplies I gave you."

"Yes, but it took some doing over the past few days. I got everything on the list; even salt water soap. There's a lot of preserved meat aboard, but I'm hoping we will have fresh fish now and then."

"Oh we will, with any luck, but you have to be prepared for the worst. Clyde and I were out for two weeks once and never caught a fish. I'll take the helm while you eat your lunch."

Rodger took Helen's place on the cockpit's bench seat and ate from the tray. "Really? I had no idea fish were that scarce."

"They didn't used to be, but that was before the dams on the spawning rivers and tributaries were built. Also commercial pollution and large trawler fish-processing ships took a great toll. Japan and Russia can take credit for much of that carnage."

"What a shame. Maybe we'll luck out; I'd really like a more varied diet than canned meat." As he sat eating his lunch he let his eyes scan the passing scene. "I feel the wind picking up, the waves are higher and our hull speed seems to be increasing."

Helen smiled, "You know Rodg, you're talking and acting more like a sailor even in this short time. You even look more like a sailor, more color in your face and your eyes look more alive."

"Wow! I'm not used to compliments like that; maybe I've missed my calling all these years. Perhaps I should have been a sailor instead of a mortgage broker." Rodger's face shone with pleasure from the conversation.

"So that's what you did for a living, sounds like something I'd have no interest in. But what do I know about the banking world, I was a physical education teacher before I married Clyde."

"Really? Did you and Clyde have children?"

"No. I was the typical old maid schoolteacher. I didn't marry until I was nearly fifty years old and beyond my childbearing years. Clyde and I only had ten years together, but he taught me to be a sailor. I only sold the boat because I couldn't comfortably single-hand it. There never was anyone to crew for me, so I'm enjoying this as much as you are." Helen stood at the tiller enjoying the comaraderie of the moment. "Look, there's Point-No-Point ahead to port, and by the looks of the water up there, I'd say we're in for stronger wind as soon as we round the point. It often blows down Admiralty Inlet like water in a funnel. In addition to that, the current can run up to four knots."

"You don't look like an old maid school teacher, Skipper. I'd say you looked more like a mature woman athlete of some outdoor sport, perhaps like sailing, swimming or skiing."

"I'll take that as a compliment, but don't emphasize the word mature too strongly, I'm not ready for the scrap heap yet. I figure I have ten active years left in me; then I'll play at the sedentary life." Helen stood a little taller warming up to the compliment.

Rodger felt the formality of their relationship easing into a friendship. "I guess I'm retired for all practical purposes because of my health problem. I wish I could say I had ten active years left; it would take a miracle. My doctor has given me a year. Actually, I'd settle for one good active year. That would get me to Tahiti and time to settle into island life. Then I'd be ready to play at the sedentary life, only mine would really be sedentary."

Helen was silent for a moment. "Who knows?" Her voice softening, "this trip might just be the making of you."

The lull in their conversation gave Rodger an opportunity to drink in the beauty of their surroundings. As they approached Point No Point, the huge expanse of water opened up even wider. Rodger remembered reading somewhere this being a meeting place of the ocean water coming down the Straits of Juan de Fuca and the ocean water coming down the inside passage between Vancouver Island and British Columbia.

Helen became intent on her task at the helm as the point neared. "When we round the point we'll be on a compass setting of 310 degrees, and on a starboard reach. If we aren't ready for the change, we could get a knock down and we sure don't want that." Breaking waves ahead indicated shallow water causing her to swing the bow to starboard to skirt the Point. Helen shouted to Rodger, "Slack off the sails," as the rail went underwater. Once around the Point, she swing the bow to port to the new heading while Rodger repeat the sail tending.

Once they're on an even keel again, Rodger plopped down beside Helen. "O.K. Skipper, I can guess what a knock down is, but a starboard reach is beyond me."

Helen smiles at Rodger's comment, then assumes an instructor's role. "When the wind is coming over the starboard side of the hull, which of course puts your sails to portside and you are holding that course for a while, you are on a starboard reach."

"I don't know Skipper, there's a lot to learn in just the vocabulary of sailing. I am beginning to feel like I've never been on a boat before, which isn't true."

"Cheer up mate, give it a little time. If I use a word or phrase you don't understand, ask me. After all, none of us is born with a vocabulary and now we use thousands of words."

"All right Skipper, your point is well taken; I'll just learn and enjoy. I'm glad you're an experienced teacher, you're going to get an opportunity to use all of your skills with me. Where do you plan for us to stay tonight?"

"Port Ludlow would be a full day's run, and it's only an hour and a half ahead of us if this wind holds. If not, we'll motor in and find moorage for the night. We can use the guest dock to tie up or just drop anchor in the bay. What would you like to do, Rodg? It's your boat."

"I'd like to drop anchor and see what it's like to be isolated on a boat over a period longer than a few hours. Tomorrow night we can look for dockside moorage. How does that sound?"

"Sounds like a plan, Mate. By the way, did you notice the current is going the same direction as we? It adds to our total speed. Being close-hauled, our hull speed is about six knots, so, if the current is four knots and the hull speed is 6 knots, we are moving across the land below us at 10 knots. That's excellent time for a sailboat."

"I feel like we're doing twice that speed. What does close-hauled mean?"

"Close-hauled means you have winched down the jib, main, and mizzen sheets as tight as you can without running water over the rail, while still keeping the tell-tales parallel."

"Thanks for the lesson, Skipper. I think I see Port Ludlow ahead; your navigating is right on target. By the way, I've noticed the current seems to divide here and part of it is going to port."

"That's because we're passing the mouth of Hood Canal. It's a natural canal shaped like a giant fish hook eighty miles long and up to two miles wide. It takes a lot of water to fill up. A few more minutes and we will be beyond the rip tides, whirl pools, and rolling water caused by Hood

Canal's entrance. If you look ahead you can see relatively flat water in the bay at Port Ludlow."

"It's been a wonderful day, Skipper."

"It's only the beginning, Mate!"

✻   ✻   ✻   ✻

CHAPTER 2

▼

Sitting at the drop leaf table in the salon, Helen studied the navigation chart detailing the harbor at Port Ludlow, their first port of call. Rodger, stationed at the helm, let his mind drift back over the past few hours. *This had been a full day starting at Des Moines marina and will end at the marina in Port Ludlow. According to Helen, that's a distance of forty nautical miles. We've averaged five miles per hour, which is a respectable performance for a sailboat, I'm told.*

Rodger scanned the waters ahead for obstacles. He liked the powerful feeling of having command of this nine-ton vessel, the Sea Witch. It made him feel like an intricate and all-important part of this whole sailing phenomenon. In this state of euphoria he relaxed at the tiller and let his mind wander back to his inner life. *I wonder what the family's reaction was to my letter. There will have been phone calls today from Irene, to our three sons at the least. They'll be concerned because I'm ill and running away to attempt this monumental adventure, which they'll consider foolhardy. Being in good health and a knowledgeable sailor is one thing, but they know I'm neither. I wonder if they'll try to stop me by alerting the Coast Guard, or police, or both? But what would the charge be...dementia?*

I told them in my letter I had arranged for the previous owner to act as Skipper, companion, and nurse, if a nurse be needed. Does this sound like the act of a demented person? They'll probably assume the previous owner of the Sea Witch is a man, few woman own sailboats, or sail for that matter. When I keep my promise to make a phone call at our first port-of-call, the truth will be known, if I identify Helen as the skipper. This may make Irene angry enough to try to stop me. Rodger looked up at the tell-tales near the top of the mainsail to be sure the sailing attitude of the Sea Witch was correct, that's what the tell-tales were for. The two narrow strips of nylon, one on each side near the top of the mainsail was parallel, as they should be. This told him the wind pressure was equal on each side of the sail. Satisfied, he scanned forward on their path ahead for obstacles. Finding none he reverted to his reverie. *What happened to Irene and me? After thirty years of marriage how and why did our relationship deteriorate over the past few years? We started out like most couples, happy, in love, seeking the good life, which included children, a home, a place in the community, financial security. We've had it all, but now after thirty years we're no longer lovers, only friends. Is that the way of marriage? I'll have to give Helen's identity issue more thought before I make that phone call. If I don't go ashore at Port Ludlow I won't have to make it, will I?"*

Helen appeared out of the companionway, "It looks like the wind is slackening; it usually does once you're past Tala Point. I'll take the tiller while you start the engine, we'll do better now under power."

"Aye, aye, Captain," replied Rodger, thankful to be interrupted from his train of thought.

Turning the tiller over to Helen, he went below to coax the engine into life. It was a get-down-on-your-hands-and-knees kind of job. Priming the engine, he pulled the flywheel through by use of a spring loaded pull rope, and the engine sputtered to life. Returning to the cockpit just as Helen was bringing the Sea Witch into the wind, he moved quickly to the mast, uncleated the halyard and dropped the jib.

"Good job Rodg, stow the jib in the sail bag later and we'll leave it on deck attached to the deck cleat. Release the halyard for the mainsail and let's flake, or fold, it on top of the boom as it comes down. Take the tiller, I'll show you how to use the sail line to wrap the mainsail to the boom." She stepped aside to make room for Rodger to take the tiller. "That puts it out of the way and ready for use tomorrow. Now we'll do the same with the mizzen sail."

The wind had died completely by the time they entered the bay that lay beyond Tala Point. Port Ludlow appeared to be a good choice for the night and finding a place to drop anchor was no problem. Helen carefully guided the Sea Witch through a maze of larger boats and settled for a spot a hundred yards off shore. Rodger's gaze swept the harbor and surrounding area teaming with people, boats, and condominiums.

"August is the prime month for the boating crowd in the Northwest," explained Helen, "brings them out in full force."

"It's only five o'clock," commented Rodger. "We should have time to relax or take a row in the dingy before dinner. By the way, what do you have in mind for dinner?"

"That's your department Rodg. Whatever you want to fix is what we'll eat. I told you, I don't really like to cook and I'm not a fussy eater. If you're out for a row in the dinghy you might try your hand at fishing; these bays usually have bottom fish, if nothing else."

"Great idea! There's a small pole on board, so I'm off to catch dinner."

Rodger abandoned his sweater almost immediately and now removed his T-shirt exposing his slender, pale upper body. *Maybe the warm sun will combat this demon in me,* he thought. *If I can just stay positive about this thing, I think I can prove the doctors wrong. They say a year if I take care of myself, meaning mostly bed rest. Yet, today is glorious and I feel more alive now then I have in months. Even if they are right, I've had today. Death, you really are the sugar of life; today is so sweet.*

Helen moved quickly about the cabin stowing her gear in the spaces she knew so well. Because Rodger stowed his gear in the forward berth area, she could see that he meant for her to have the divan in the salon for sleeping. The galley, small but adequate, took up the rest of the space except for a passageway leading to the small diesel engine under the cockpit floor. The drop-leaf table in the middle of the salon was the catchall for maps, books, etc. and most importantly, a place to prepare and serve food. At the end of the day it was moved out of the way to make room for the hide-a-bed divan.

Helen leaned back on the familiar berth and remembered when she and Clyde had shared this salon. Her mind tracing back over the day came to rest on Rodger. *He is basically a very decent sort of guy forced to look at the end of life's journey too soon and ask himself, "Is that all there is?" He's evidently decided to squeeze the most he can get out of these last few months of his life. That's where I came in. Was it just a spur-of-the-moment decision when I offered to skipper the Sea Witch to Tahiti? I could hardly believe what I heard myself saying. I decided to stick with my offer, but occasionally I've had feelings of anxiety. Is this a way of joining Clyde sooner? Drowning, I'm told, isn't a bad way to die and in a storm at sea would certainly be a dramatic conclusion to my full and satisfying life.*

Rodger pulled the dinghy alongside the Sea Witch and carefully lifted a freshly cleaned, three-pound salmon aboard. Tying the bowline of the dinghy to the stern cleat on the transom of the Sea Witch, he stepped aboard. "Is there anyone aboard who likes fresh salmon?" When he received no answer he headed for the cabin. "Hello, anybody home?" Poking his head inside, he found Helen lost in thought, staring off into space.

"What's that in your hand?" she exclaimed, visibly shaking herself out of her reverie. "It looks like an honest-to-goodness edible fish."

"My dear lady, this is the king of the northwest seas, a king salmon."

"Did you catch it?"

"I'm sorry you asked; I was hoping you would assume I did. Actually, I bought it for two dollars off one of the fishing boats. They had such a small catch they decided to sell to the locals instead of going to the fish buyer. After catching only a scrap fish, I decided to ensure we had fish for dinner."

"Well, Rodg, I'm pleased with your decision; I'll do my part and enjoy it."

"If I cook it on the barbeque, we won't smell up the cabin, and we can really doctor it up with sauces and spices. I'm guessing the barbeque fits in that piece of hardware connected to the gunnels near the transom. Gunnels, transom; now if that language doesn't sound nautical, nothing does."

"You know, Rodg, I'm going to make a sailor out of you yet. By the way, I'm up for an Old English 800; I'll drink beer and you cook dinner. How does that sound?"

"What's wrong with this picture?" Rodger laughed as he reached into the cooler, handed Helen a beer, and then retreated to the galley. Climbing the steps topside, Helen decided stretch out on the foredeck and enjoy the early evening solitude. The harbor noises were diminishing as workers were now on their way home. Boaters were busy showering and cleaning up for the traditional cocktail hour preceding dinner with the yachting class. The rhythmic lap of the waves on the hull and the strong beer lulled Helen into a welcome nap after a busy day.

Rodger had assembled the barbeque over the stern of the boat, filled it with briquettes, dowsed them with starter fluid, and lit it with his propane lighter. Satisfied with the briquettes, he retreated to the galley to prepare the salmon. Cutting off its head, he split the fish down the middle, laying it lay out like two extended hands and placed it on a bed of aluminum foil twice the dimensions of the fish. He then cut a dry onion and a lemon into thin slices and carefully placed them on the open fish. Tucking the edges of the aluminum foil up so it would hold liquid, he went topside to place it on the barbeque.

While the fish cooked, he opened a loaf of French bread, wrapped it in aluminum foil, and added it to the grill. Seasoning the cooking salmon with a mixture of spices blended for seafood, he closed the aluminum foil that held the salmon. After making a green salad, Rodger selected a Riesling wine and put it on ice in the small icebox. He decided to scrape and cut carrots, wrapped also in aluminum foil and placed along side the salmon.

Returning topside to check on the barbeque, Rodger noticed Helen dozing on the foredeck. *She is really quite a gal,* he mused. *She's not nearly as domineering or dogmatic as she had seemed at first.* I hope she'll be able to put aside Clyde's ghost. Being on board the Sea Witch seems to have brought back memories of their sailing days together; I'm sure they were happy ones.

Rodger settled into the cockpit where he could periodically inspect the salmon on the barbeque. Leafing through the ship's log, he was determined to know more about the Sea Witch and her beginnings. It seems Eli Johnson, a professional boat builder near Tracyton, Washington had built her in 1947. It said John Hanna had drawn the plans for a Tahiti Ketch in 1923 and an unknown number of them had been built between then and the late forties. The plans that came with the Sea Witch showed her to be 30 feet long from stem to stern with a 10-foot beam.

She draws four feet of water and weighs in at nine tons. Massively built with solid oak keel, stem, and oak frames, she's fir planked. Her spars are all solid spruce and she carries 470 square feet of sail.

"Oh, she's a solid oceangoing boat, for sure," he'd been told by the marine surveyor Rodger'd hired to do the survey before he bought her.

Rodger had to admit he was first attracted to the Sea Witch because she bore the design name of his intended destination, Tahiti. According to the surveyor the design was called the Neptune for the first twelve years of its existence, but later changed to Tahiti when it caught the fancy of backyard boat builders worldwide. *This is not a boat,* it occurred to Rodger, *it's a ship because of its design and the way it handles.*

Helen stirred, raised herself on one elbow. "How's dinner coming, chef? I think I'm about ready to do justice to your 'fresh caught' salmon."

"Well Captain, if you'll set the table and pour yourself a glass of wine, it should be ready to serve by then."

"You're in charge," replied Helen as she made her way back to the cockpit, and descended down the ladder to the salon. Putting up the sides on the drop leaf table, and moving about quickly as one adept at living aboard, she set the table. Then she poured herself a glass of wine.

* * * *

CHAPTER 3

▼

After dinner, Helen volunteered to cleanup while Rodger, sitting in the shadows of the day's ending, smoked his nightly pipe on deck. *Our relationship will be growing each day with this adventure,* he thought. *It's so challenging to both of us. If my health improves as we travel, I'll see Tahiti. If Helen survives the ghostly return of her husband, she'll see Tahiti. If the weather stays favorable and the Sea Witch holds together, we'll see Tahiti. If the authorities don't stop us for whatever reason that Irene might trump up, we'll see Tahiti. So many ifs' and only time will tell which ifs' will apply.*

Finishing his pipe, Rodger checked the lines to the dinghy and anchor. The mooring light was lit on at the top of the mast and all seemed well. As he went below to the salon, Helen emerged from the bathroom. *Now comes the cozy part.* "Helen, I'll use the head and then close the curtains to my forward bunk area. That way you'll have the privacy of the salon."

"That should work, Rodg. I'll go topside and check things there and enjoy the evening air."

When Helen returned Rodger was in his bunk asleep; it had been a full day for both of them. Helen stretched out her sleeping bag on the divan and went through her evening ritual at the sink. This didn't match her accommodations at home, but in a way this was her second home. In her eyes this was still her and Clyde's boat even though she had sold it to Rodger.

Rodger was the perfect one to buy it, being at death's door. It's a win-win situation for me; if we make it to Tahiti, it will be a great adventure and accomplishment; if we're lost at sea, I'll rejoin my beloved Clyde. For Rodg, it will be win-win, too. If we make it to Tahiti, he will have achieved his life-long fantasy; if we don't make it, he won't have to go through the awful final stages of tuberculosis. Helen lie there a long time staring at the interior of the salon, aware of the gentle rocking of the boat, listening to the lapping sound of the waves against the hull. Finally sleep covered her like a comfortable blanket easing her mind of what lie ahead.

Rodger awoke first, taking a few seconds to get his bearings. The previous day came into focus causing him to smile at what they had accomplished so far. Rolling out of his sleeping bag, he pulled on yesterday's clothes thinking how good it would be to have a shower. Grabbing clean underwear and socks, he searched his pocket change for quarters. If this marina is like other marinas, there will be facilities ashore for showering, laundry, etc. He quietly tiptoed through the salon noticing Helen looking so peaceful in sleep on the divan. After leaving a note, he cast off in the dinghy and rowed to the dock.

It was 7:00 a.m. and only a few people were visible, mostly delivery workers. Rodger spotted the shower area near the harbormaster's office. Finding an open shower, he enjoyed the warm water washing over his slender body. He took advantage of the hot water to shave, shampoo, and then resisted a cold water wash down. Spasms of deep, body-wracking coughing reminded him of his illness, although he felt more alive now than he had in a long time.

Leaving the men's shower room, he noticed two pay phones immediately opposite the exit door. Should he or should he not make the promised phone call? He decided he wasn't ready to talk to Irene thus giving her a chance to talk him out of his adventure, or have her call the authorities to stop him against his will. *I don't know if the authorities can do that, but I don't want to take a chance. I'll postpone calling for at least another day. In the meantime I'll picked up the morning paper and head back to the Sea Witch.*

As he pulled alongside in the dinghy he could tell by the sounds and aroma from the galley Helen was up and had coffee on. Tying the dinghy bow line to the stern cleat, he pushed it away from the Sea Witch to avoid the two bumping together. The hatch door was open and below lay his new home. "Hi. I see you're usurping my roll as chief cook and galley slave."

"When I discovered you abandoned ship, I knew if I was going to have my wake-up coffee, I'd better fix it. You look trim, did you find a shower?"

"I did, and it was wonderful. It's funny how our priorities change when we change our daily lives. I highly recommend the public spa located near the harbormaster's office; I'll even spring for the cost of a shower."

"How can I refuse an offer like that?" replied Helen. "Now, if I can interest you in my style of morning coffee, we can lay out our plans for the day. I'm thinking Port Angeles would be a good day's sail assuming the wind is in our favor and we're moving with the current."

"What's the weather forecast?"

"The forecast is for temperatures from 48 to 72 degrees today with variable winds northerly at 5 to 15 knots with a rising barometer. The tide change is at 9:20 and we'll have an outgoing tide."

"Sounds like a great day for sailing. It's 8:05 now, unless you take extra long showers, we should be on our way by tide change," ventured Rodger as he moved toward the galley.

"I'll take my coffee with me to the showers; you fix breakfast and I'll be back by 8:40. And by the way, I like my eggs medium, my bacon well done, and my toast lightly buttered."

"Really?" Rodger chuckled as he moved to pour himself a mug of coffee. Sitting down to read the morning paper he thought, *I wonder how the market is doing this morning? Hmmm. Interest rates are falling. That's good, as a lot of people will want to refinance their mortgages. That should make Irene happy.*

* * * *

Irene paced the floor in the living room as she waited impatiently for her oldest son, Rodger, Jr. to appear. She had waited until breakfast time to call him. *No sense in Junior having to put in a night like I've had. How could Rodger do such a fool-heardy thing? Imagine going off to Tahiti in a 30 foot sailboat when he's at death's door. The only sensible thing about it is that he hired an experienced skipper to sail the 'stupid' boat. I hate the ocean, I don't like boats, and I prefer my outings in small doses; not like Rodger.*

Junior's car pulled into the circular driveway. Jumping out, he slammed the car door and headed for the house on the run. "Mother, where are you?"

"I'm in the living room, dear." Irene was seated on the Louis V loveseat. Both its elegance and that of the lovely Christian Dior negligee she wore reflected the luxury and good taste of the large, luxurious lifestyle room.

Junior, a larger man than his father with similar English features, could see the stress in his mother's face caused by worry and lack of sleep. "Well, what's the old man done this time? You said something about a boat and Tahiti over the phone."

"Here, read this letter he pinned to my pillow; I noticed it when I got ready for bed last night. I thought he was just late getting home from his day trip to Portland; instead this!"

Junior rolled his eyes as he read the letter and handed it back to his mother. "I can't believe he would do this. Although, it's not too far out of character for him. The flying lessons when he turned forty, the motorcycle when he turned fifty, and now this when sixty is just around the corner. Surely you're going to stop him, if for no other reason than it's suicide?"

"That was my first impulse, however, after thinking about it, I wonder if this isn't a dying man's wish. I want what's best for him, and the doctor has only given him six months to a year to live. He's approached me about the two of us sailing to Tahiti some time ago. I told him, no way would I do that. I guess this is his way of getting what he wants with what's left of his life."

"Yes, but he could be lost at sea and no insurance for you for seven years, if his body isn't found. That's a big ocean out there, and he's not that much of a sailor. He could even die of tuberculosis on his way to Tahiti for lack of hospital care. It sounds like the act of a desperate man."

"Of course dear, it's the act of a dying man. One who is desperate to do this last life-fulfilling fantasy. Evidently, he's willing to go out of this life violently, if need be. When he arrives in Tahiti, he said he would send for me. I think I could handle his death at sea as well as I could handle his death in a hospital or sanitarium, and I'm no Florence Nightingale."

"It doesn't sound like you need my opinion, Mother. It sounds like you've already made a decision."

"Yes dear, I guess I have. Now, let's have some breakfast and go to the office. Mortgage rates are falling, business should be good."

* * * *

Rodger started frying the eggs as soon as he heard the dingy bump against the side of the Sea Witch. Now he quickly put the cooked bacon and toast on the table and poured two mugs of steaming hot coffee. By the time Helen started down the ladder to the salon he had the medium-over eggs on two plates and was half way to the table.

"Wow! I'm impressed. Are you sure you're not too good to be real?"

"Well, I am working on perfection, but, I'll admit, I'm not quite there yet. This is one of my better performances; let's eat and enjoy it."

After eating every last crumb, they stowed the dishes in the sink until later. Rodger started the engine, unflaked the sails then raised them, then raised the anchor as the Sea Witch started to move forward under its own sail power.

"I thought we would start the day by leaving the harbor under sail and using the auxiliary engine if needed," half-shouted Helen as Rodger cleared the foredeck and secured the whisker pole. "It's a good time to practice close-quarters maneuvering when we have ideal conditions to do it. When we get into the straits we'll sail wing and wing if the wind continues from our stern. If it changes to a northwesterly, we'll go on a beat at that time."

"O.K., I give up. What's wing and wing?" asked Rodger with a ghost of a smile creasing the corners of his mouth. "And what's a beat?"

"When the wind is aft, wing and wing means that the mainsail is out on one side of the hull and the jib sail on the opposite side," Helen explained as she scanned ahead to avoid boats and buoys. "From the stern it looks like two wings even though the mainsail is larger than the jib and more aft."

"That makes sense, but the main has a boom to hold the bottom of the sail rigid, whereas the jib doesn't. How do you control the jib?" asked Rodger with a perplexed look.

"That's where the whisker pole comes in. It's like a small boom that we attach to the hardware called a cringle at the bottom of the jib and to a fitting on the mast. That way we get the most out of the sail. You asked about a beat," continued Helen as she carefully maneuvered among the anchored boats on their way out of the bay. "A beat is like we were trimmed yesterday when we rounded Point No Point, remember? The jib, mizzen, and mainsails were winched down tight and we were heeled over up to the point where the rail or gunnels was almost running in the water?"

"Yes, I remember the beat, and now I know what a whisker pole is for."

"We've worked our way out of Port Ludlow past Tala Point; now we'll take a course heading of 330 degrees, which is north, northwest. This part of Puget Sound is called Admiralty Inlet and leads to the Straits of Juan De Fuca." Helen checked the full, billowing sails. "The wind is holding and out of the southwest, which puts it over the stern. We can sail wing and wing for now and change sail position or jibe as we round Pt. Wilson, which is a ways up ahead. The weatherman promises a temperature high of 72 degrees, which is ideal for the straits," she added.

"Let's see, cringle is hardware, clew is the bottom aft corner of the sail and jibe is when the mainsail boom goes from port to starboard or vice versa."

"Right! Now, sit here by me and watch how I handle the boat wing and wing."

"Aye, aye, Captain." Rodger moved back in the cockpit and sat on the bench seat near Helen. "What time do you think we'll get into Port Angeles?"

"If the wind holds and we can shift from wing and wing at Pt. Wilson to a close-hauled reach, I would estimate about five o'clock. That will give us time to clean up at the marina and walk into town. There is a Thai restaurant there I like and it may be our last chance to get a good restaurant meal for awhile. Neah Bay, our next stop, has only one restaurant and it doesn't meet my standards."

The farther north they sail the fewer houses are seen along the shore. The trees, mostly Douglas Fir, Cedar, and Madronna, came right down to the high tide mark where bleached driftwood in all possible shapes adorn the beach. Seagulls, circle, dive, and feed on the herring balls that appear on and near the surface of the water. Sport fishermen in small kicker boats follow and troll near the diving, screeching birds; it is summer in the beautiful Northwest.

"This wing and wing is great. The wind coming over the stern enables us to sail on a pretty even keel, doesn't it?"

"That's right, Mate. Would you take the tiller for a while? I'd like to go below and clean up the galley. After all, you fixed breakfast."

"Sure, I'll take the helm, but you're the captain and I expect to do the dishes, along with cooking the meals, and making myself generally useful."

"Well, Rodg, fair is fair. I'll teach you all I know about sailing the Sea Witch, but I would like it to be an equal endeavor. We each share the helm and we each share the work. Except that you cook and I clean up. Is that agreeable?"

"Sounds good to me. I'll do my best to be a good student. Who knows? Our lives may depend on it."

Helen retreated to the salon below and busied herself with the breakfast dishes. As she worked she mentally brought herself up-to-date. *Rodger is all that he appears to be. Honest, energetic, friendly, and a man with a dream, a dream with a time limit. How sad he can't live to really enjoy Tahiti, assum-*

ing we get there. I sometimes feel so close to Clyde, like right now when I'm in the galley and the Sea Witch is sailing along without me being on deck. It's like Clyde is up there at the tiller.

"Hey Helen, would you put the coffee pot on? I could use a cup of your famous coffee."

Helen moved over to the open hatch, walked up three steps, and stuck her head out of the cabin to say, "Roger wilco."

"What is this Roger wilco jazz?"

"That's a term from my Army days, which fits this occasion and probably a lot more before this journey is completed. Roger, means O.K. and wilco, means I will comply."

"You were in the Army?" Asked Rodger incredulously. "What else haven't you told me?"

"I served four years in the U.S. Army during the Viet Nam police action as a drill instructor for W.A.C.'s at one of the basic training centers."

"I should have suspected," grinned Rodger.

"About the rest of my life, that will come on a need-to-know basis."

* * * *

CHAPTER 4

▼

Rodger stood at the tiller and sucked in the day while he waited for his coffee. *This is great, I can't believe life can be this good. Especially after the depression I've felt after the doctor's last pronouncement; "six months to a year, so do what's important to you." If this trip isn't doing what's important to me, I don't know what is? I hope Irene and the boys will accept what I'm doing. I want their approval, but I don't have to have it. I think I'm ready to make that phone call now when we hit port. I want to make this as easy for them as I can. However, I don't know if I'm ready to tell them the skipper is a woman.*

As long as Helen and my relationship is platonic, I really don't think it's necessary to burden my family with that fact. Helen is becoming a real friend and our relationship has changed. However, no one likes a sick cat and that's what I am, so I don't see any change beyond platonic. She's quite a woman, I'm finding out, and I hope I can be as helpful for her as she is for me.

Helen emerged from the hatch with a mug of coffee in each hand. "Here's your order Mate, do you want sugar?"

"No thanks, I'll just stir it with my thumb."

"Really?" Helen laughed.

Rising to the occasion of light heartedness, "My next line is 'as all us loggers do.' Have you heared that Northwest Ballad?"

"As a matter of fact, I have. My father was a logger. He used to sing it to me and when I was a little girl. He'd bellow out the line, 'I can tell that you're a logger, because you stir your coffee with your thumb'. Then I'd follow with a stanza, 'My lover was a logger, there's none like him today. If you'd pour some gravy on it, he'd eat a bale of hay.'"

"Such fun!" replied Rodger. "Maybe we should change that from logger to sailor and have it for our theme song. Have you noticed the wind has changed direction and is freshening out of the North? Maybe we'll get to Port Angeles sooner than your E.T.A."

"I was just going to suggest that we go off wing and wing, Rodg. I'll take in the whisker pole and let the jib work naturally. There, notice it's slack now, so I'll trim the jib sheet and let it fill. Notice the list of the hull has changed and we're heeling to port. The wind is filling our sails differently now as both of them are out on the same side of the hull. With this set the sails are brought in much tighter, and the tell-tales on the upper part of the sail are parallel."

"Hold it, Helen. Tell me about telltales again. I feel like I'm getting too much information too fast."

"Sorry about that Mate. I keep forgetting what you don't know. Do you see those two pieces of nylon yarn fastened to the top leading edge of the mainsail?"

Rodger leaned back to look at the telltales on the sail. "Yes, one is on this side of the sail and one is on the other side of the sail, which we see only as a shadow."

"Right. Let me take the tiller and notice what happens when I fall off the wind a few degrees. See how the telltales are no longer parallel."

"Oh, yeah. The telltale on the backside is drooping while the other stays the way it was. What does that tell us?"

"It tells us that the sail isn't trimmed right in accordance with the direction of the wind and the direction we're steering the boat. The wind is not of equal velocity on each side of the sail. We either have to change the direction of the boat or we have to trim or ease the sail setting. However, you usually trim the sail to the wind because you have a destination and the bow is pointed the way you want to go."

"Boy, there sure is a lot to learn in this sailing business. I had no idea how much when I thought about sailing to Tahiti. What on earth would I ever do without you?"

"Frankly, Mate, you'd still be in Poverty Bay where we started."

Rodger winced and changed the subject. "I notice we're off Point Wilson according to the chart. I guess a new compass heading will be needed."

A whole new body of water opens up ahead as they pass Point Wilson. They leave Admiralty Inlet behind and enter the Straits of Juan de Fuca. Fifty nautical miles north across this vast open water crossroads lies Canada's Vancouver Island with the large city of Vancouver visible at its very southern tip. After having traveled through the smaller waterways of Puget Sound with its many islands and fjords, this large expanse of water is like an inland sea. The American and Canadian San Juan Islands lie to starboard and east of Vancouver Island. The Olympic Peninsula, with the stately Olympic Mountains towering over the Straits of Juan de Fuca, lies to port paralleling the Sea Witch's journey route.

Cargo ships of the world pass each other with imports from the Orient and Europe coming inbound mostly to Seattle and Tacoma, Washington, and exports outbound, to provide a balance of trade, come from these same two seaports. Tankers from Alaska's northern slope and the Mid East are in the shipping lanes too, loaded to the gunnels with crude and refined oil; they return empty. Cruise ships, mostly bound for Alaska or returning, like majestic floating hotels, are a recent addition to the parade of vessels. Pleasure craft of every description fill in the blank spaces on the open water, passing through the shipping lanes quickly, as they don't argue with the commercial giants for right-of-way.

"Our new heading will be 290 degrees," stated Helen as she relaxed at the helm. "This setting we'll hold until we clear Dungeness Spit. Then we'll ease off to a heading of 250 degrees, which will bring us into the windward side of Edez Hook and into Port Angeles, now that the wind has changed from southwest to north."

Rodger also relaxed and enjoyed lying back on the bench seat to take advantage of the noontime sun. The public marina next to the ferry dock lay ahead with its twenty transient slips for the convenience of the summer boaters. "Are you ready for one of my famous Spam sandwiches and a cool Old English?" he asked.

"That's music to my ears, Rodg. A few chips and a pickle would go well, Spam needs all the help it can get."

Rodger went below and spread out the food ingredients on the drop leaf table. In short order he had two sandwiches, two beers, two large dill pickles, and a handful of potato chips spread on a paper towel. Carefully making his way balancing the tray of food and drink up to the cockpit he called out, "Okay, Skipper, I'll take the tiller while you eat unencumbered for a change."

"Thanks Rodg." Immediately making her way forward, she spread the lunch beside her on the foredeck making the most of the summer day. The cumulonimbus clouds overhead reminded her of mare's tails the way they swept across the sky. God's handiwork fairly took her breath away. *This day makes up for a lot of gray days I've had this past year; maybe life is worth living after all. It's great being back on the Sea Witch. It's just too bad Rodger has tuberculosis as he really is a nice companion, and who knows what the future could hold?*

Rodger, sitting at the helm, felt the pressure of the tiller in his hand each time the hull dove into the gentle swells of the straits. *The tell-tales are parallel,* he thought, *the main, jib and mizzen are trimmed just right according to the tell-tales, and the Sea Witch is in her glory. All seems right with the world, and tonight I think I'll call Irene.*

"There's the end of Edez Hook at eleven o'clock," called out Helen.

"What's this eleven o'clock jazz?"

Gathering the remains of her lunch, she returned to the cockpit, "That's army talk, here's how it works. Think of a large clock face lying on the surface of the water and picture that the bow of the boat points to twelve o'clock. If I say look at eleven o'clock, then you would look off to the left of twelve o'clock to about where eleven o'clock would be on this huge clock face. Try it, see if you don't see something at eleven o'clock."

"Oh yeah, I see what you mean. There's a lighthouse on a narrow spit of land. Although, I would say it looks more like ten-thirty."

"Yeah, now!" replied Helen, playing along with the tease. "When we get within a hundred yards off the point, change the compass heading to 250 degrees, that should bring us to the transient dock and an afternoon nap."

"Sounds like a plan, Skipper."

"Do you see that ferry dock in the middle of the harbor shoreline?" asked Helen as she pointed straight ahead. "Just to the left of it is the observation pier for the locals and the tourists and to the left of that is the transient dock. I'll take the tiller while you go below and start the engine; then we can drop the sails."

"Aye, aye Skipper."

"I'll bring the bow into the wind so you can drop the jib, mizzen, and mainsail. The engine will make this an easy, upwind approach. I've picked out a slip, go forward and handle the lines as we coast in. When you secure a bowline, I'll secure the stern with a line to the dock cleat. We'll then set up a spring line."

"I know how to set a spring line," stated Rodger.

Helen shifted into neutral and eyed the approaching finger pier in order to coast in close so Rodger could step off at just the right moment and secure them.

Helen, standing at the tiller, held the course and watched the hull slide gently up to the finger pier. Rodger stepped briskly off the Sea Witch onto the dock, as Helen leaned over the gunnels with a stern line in hand to throw a double half hitch around the rear cleat. Rodger followed suit and moored the bow in the same manner. He thought to himself; *at least I know how to secure a boat to a dock and how to set up a spring line.*

"Well done, Mate; I couldn't have done better myself," stated Helen as she stepped off the Sea Witch onto the dock

"Thanks, Skipper. I'll run a spring line by going with a line from the stern dock cleat to the amidships deck cleat and back to the stern deck cleat. Then we can go ashore, as I'm really up for a walk. How about you?"

Helen inspected the three lines securing the boat and joined Rodger as they headed toward the gangplank up to the main dock. "I'm for that, but first, we'll have to go to the harbormaster and get moorage for the night. I think they charge fifteen dollars here."

"I'll take care of that while you talk to the people at customs. I see the two offices are side-by-side in the building beyond the ferry dock. By the way, where does the ferry go?"

"To the city of Victoria across the bay on Vancouver Island. Ever been there?"

"Yes, but I approached it from the south by way of Anacortes and through the San Juan Islands. That is a great trip, by the way."

"Let's take care of the business at hand, and when you're through I'll meet you outside the Harbor Master's office," replied Helen as she headed toward the custom office.

Rodger discovered the Harbor Master had left for the day even though it was just five o'clock. His secretary handled the transaction and they were secure for the night with a check-out time at five o'clock the next afternoon. Rodger encountered Helen just as she walked out of the customs office. "What did you find out about leaving the United States?"

"It depends on our voyage plan. If we're headed to the Hawaiian Islands from the Washington coast we can go through customs here. If we're going down the coast to California and then further south to the islands we can use customs at San Diego."

"What is our voyage plan? I've been meaning to ask you, but there has been so many other things to consider until now, it didn't seem too important."

"It's up to you Rodger; this is your boat. My choice would be to hug the Pacific coast all the way to Peru and pick up the South Equatorial Current. That would take us to the Tuomotu Archipelago and Tahiti, which is one of the Islands. Another way would be to catch the North Equatorial Current out of San Francisco and head south of the Hawaiian Islands, but that way we have to contend with the Doldrums and the Equatorial Counter Current as we work our way south to Tahiti."

"Wow! This is an important decision. If you want to hug the coast to Peru, that's what we'll do. I've never been pleasure boating out of the Puget Sound or the San Juan Islands."

"Neither have I, Mate, but you said you wanted this to be an adventure."

"That's true, but how do you know about the ocean currents and the doldrums and all that technical navigation information?"

"Clyde and I planned to take this trip to the Tuomotu Archipelago and Tahiti before he died. We read books on the subject and studied navigation so we could do it. I'm just glad I was an equal partner with Clyde and didn't leave all the planning and navigation to him."

"Me too," said Rodger as they headed up the sidewalk to downtown Port Angeles. "I'm with you all the way, Skipper."

"Thanks for the vote of confidence, Rodg. If we don't make it, I'll give you a refund on your ticket," bantered Helen.

"I'm pleased to know I have such an ironclad guarantee." Spasms of coughing ended his gales of laughter at the acknowledgement by Helen of her limited expertise. The coughing did help bring their situation back into perspective.

Helen gently took his hand as they continued walking together. It was early afternoon and a fair number of tourists filled the sidewalk. This was the older part of town, and the old stores had become new businesses that catered to the wants and needs of tourists. Arriving at the Indonesian restaurant Helen recommended, Rodger broke the light-hearted spell by announcing he had a phone call to make to his family back in Seattle.

* * * *

"Irene, this is Rodger."

"Where are you?" Irene's voice had a steel edge to it.

Rodger hesitated, but continued, "I'm in Port Angeles and everything is going okay. My health is no worse, the weather's fine and I'm learning how to be a sailor, not just a boater Irene. A real sailor."

"Well, isn't that wonderful," replied Irene with sarcasm. "I'm madder than hell at you, Rodger McCauley. I feel like the deserted wife and I don't understand you sneaking around buying a boat and running out on me and the family."

"I had hoped for some understanding on your part, Irene. I guess I knew you'd never understand the depth of my mental anguish that would drive me to do this," replied Rodger, disappointment filling his voice. "I'm going to continue on my journey, Irene, with or without your approval."

Irene was silent for a minute…then said, "If that's your decision, Rodger, there is nothing more to say. We both know your time is running out, and I've never had any Florence Nightingale tendencies. Call me when you start your ocean crossing."

Rodger sensed the difference in Irene's attitude. "That may be awhile; we're hugging the Pacific Coast all the way to Peru before we head into off-shore sailing. By that time I should be an accomplished sailor. My Captain says I'm a good student."

"I imagine you are, Rodger." By the way, what's your captain's name?"

"Uh…Henry, my Captain's name is Henry, and I'll call you before we leave Pereu." he hurried on. "My feelings for the family haven't changed. Tell the boys I love them and their families even though they're angry with me. Someday, if they run into this kind of circumstance in their life, they may understand."

Irene, having vented her anger, became more reasonable. "Then I'll say Bon Voyage to you and Captain Henry…and Rodger, don't pick up any mermaids."

"I'll remember that Irene. Good bye." Rodger put the phone back on its hook, breathed a long sigh of relief, and pondered his answer to Irene's question, *what's your captain's name?*

✱ ✱ ✱ ✱

"Well Rodg, did you make your phone call?" Helen walked over to where Rodger had made his call.

"Yes, I called my wife as I had promised. First she was angry and when I told her I was determined to do this, she surprised me. She wished us bon voyage."

"Really! What does she think about you traveling half way around the world with a woman, Rodg."

"Do you want the truth?"

"Of course," Helen replied closely watching at Rodger's facial expression.

"She doesn't know that; she thinks your name is Henry."

"Rodger! This could get pretty sticky somewhere down the line. I can just see her waiting at the dock in Tahiti."

"It's a complicated relationship, Helen, it's lasted this long only because neither of us had the courage to end it after the boys were grown. Habit is a strange phenomena; fear of the unknown enters the picture and unless the marriage is really uncomfortable, it's easier to do nothing."

Helen walked over to Rodger and put her arm around his shoulder. "That's sad, Rodg. It makes me wonder if your health problem is your only motivation for taking this trip to Tahiti. Maybe this is your way of handling divorce."

"My God! I hadn't made that connection…but there just may be some truth in it. If that's true, this trip to Tahiti could have a double purpose." Rodger began to pace up and down. "I think Irene and I should sit down and talk this thing out? If divorce is or isn't the choice we make, I'll feel better about this trip. I really don't like being a runaway, that's not my style under normal circumstances. However, what I've experienced so far even exceeds my expectations. You weren't in my fantasy."

Helen stopped directly in front of Rodger. "I'm shocked, Rodg. I didn't mean for my off-the-wall comment to lead to this."

"I know, but it fits. Irene and I have danced around this situation long enough. Actually, I'd feel a lot better about what I'm doing if we did talk it out and come to a decision about her and my relationship. Then I wouldn't feel like a runaway."

"What are you going to do?" Helen asked as she walked alongside along with Rodger who was headed back to the phone area.

"I'm going to call Irene back and tell her I'm flying home tomorrow. I'm going to tell her we have some decisions to make before I depart. I know this leaves you hanging, and I suggest you return to your home while Irene and I work this out. We can get moorage here at the transient dock for up to two weeks. By then everything should be resolved, and we can be on our way. I know I'll feel better about the whole trip if I do this. I won't have this guilt feeling, plus it could put a new slant on our relationship." Rodger stood holding Helen's hands in his and looking deeply into her eyes. "You are more than a skipper, more than a friend."

Helen looked pleased at Rodger's remark about their relationship, but added "I'm at a loss for words, but you're the boss. If this is what you feel you must do, then do it. I won't go home, I'll stay aboard the Sea Witch, I'm comfortable here. I like the town of Port Angeles and this shouldn't take too long. You can leave a phone message at the Harbormaster's office to let me know when you're returning. I'll check there daily until I hear from you. I know this isn't an easy decision, Rodg, but that's life isn't it?...Just a series of tough decisions."

✳ ✳ ✳ ✳

Chapter 5

▼

The next morning Rodger stepped aboard the pontoon of the floatplane bound for Seattle. In less than an hour he would be landing on Lake Union and back into his former life. The view, as he flew over the Straits of Juan de Fuca, the lower San Juan Islands, and northern Puget Sound, would normally be breathtaking, but today he was lost in his thoughts and emotions. His mission was to sit down with Irene and decide if their marriage had come to an end. If it had, what was the best way to deal with that? Was divorce the answer? Legal separation? Do nothing? His ultimate goal was to enable himself to spend his last weeks or months of life enjoying his adventure as best he could. The die was caste; he would soon know one way or another.

Leaving as he had seemed like a good idea at the time, but now he had had second thoughts. Now he knew he had to go back, face his family, and leave with their blessings if possible. He had no intention of letting them talk him out of the way he spent the rest of his life, his adventure, but he had experienced some feelings he didn't have when he started. These feelings had put him on this plane today.

How could he have known the guilt he would feel regarding running away from his wife and family? How could he have known the joy of being a sailor on his own sailboat on this adventure? How could he have known the hope he would feel about the present and the future, hope was something he hadn't felt for months. And most of all, how could he have known how he would feel about Helen?

There's Irene standing on the dock at the air terminal watching us land. Where do I begin? How do I explain what I'm feeling to my wife of thirty years from whom I feel so disconnected?

*   *   *   *

"Hello Irene thanks for meeting me."

Irene's facial expression was like a winter storm, dark and hard to read. "Hello Rodger, I didn't expect to see you so soon after your first phone call last night. Did your conscience get the best of you? Is that why you called back insisting on this meeting?"

Rodger stepped forward to touch her. She stepped away. Sensing that Irene was in a no-nonsense mood he replied, "Yes, my conscience got the best of me. I hated the thought of leaving without the family's blessing."

"We would never have given it!"

"I guess I knew that and acted accordingly."

"So why are you here, now?"

"I want to talk to you about ending our marriage, either in divorce or a legal separation."

"Oh you do, do you? Well…maybe it is time to put an end to this fiasco of a marriage."

"Let's go somewhere where we can talk," suggested Rodger. "How about Benjamin's? We can get a drink there."

"I guess that's as good a place as any; I need a drink."

Neither of them spoke as Rodger escorted Irene off the dock to their car in the nearby parking lot. Automatically going to the driver's side of the car, he realized his mistake, walked back around the car, and held out his hand for the keys.

Sensing Rodger had now turned angry, Irene opened her purse and handed him the keys without speaking. He pressed the key button opening all the doors simultaneously; they slid into their respective seats.

"What else do you have to say that you couldn't have said yesterday on the phone?"

Rodger stared out the windshield, trying to find the right words. Coming up empty he blurted, "What if I told you my skipper is a woman, a woman to whom I feel very attracted? Would that make a difference in your decision whether we go for a divorce or a legal separation, or do nothing?"

Shock sharpened Irene's voice and distorted her facial expression, "Yes, that does make a difference…is the feeling mutual…or is that any of my business? Surely she knows about your tuberculosis."

"I think the feeling is mutual, and yes, she knows."

"Boy, she must be as desperate as you are…any more surprises I need to know about?"

"No, that's it." Rodger started the car and waited for Irene to speak.

Her expression relaxed, "Let's just go home then. We can talk about it in the morning after you've had time to see the family and I've had time to think this out. The family will be over this evening for dinner."

Softening, Rodger replied, "That was nice of you to arrange dinner, Irene; I don't want us to be enemies. We've had some good years together and we have a great family; I want that to continue. I don't have a lot of time left and I want to get the most out of it, that's all. I don't want to lie around in a hospital. This trip has been a lifetime dream and Helen is a total surprise."

Her anger and shock having reached and passed their zenith, Irene sat quietly for a moment while they traveled through the Seattle traffic to their home in Bellevue. Finally she spoke, "Life hasn't been kind to you lately, Rodg, I know that. You're the one who has had to live with the pain and isolation. I wish I could have been more help to you…more loving. In a perfect world, I would have been there for you, Rodger. I guess it just isn't my nature. As I've said, I'd make a lousy Florence Nightingale."

"In a perfect world I wouldn't be dying of tuberculosis at an early age and we'd be living happily ever after," said Rodger as he stared steadily at the road ahead.

* * * *

"That was fun with the family last night, wasn't it Irene? Our daughters-in-law were a little stand-off-ish at first; I guess they don't want to face this kind of a dilemma a few years down the road. I assured them tuberculosis wasn't a gene thing and the doctor says I'm not contagious, now."

"The grandchildren look upon you as a real adventurer with your own sailboat on the way to Tahiti," added Irene. "I saw no need to share with the family that your skipper is a woman. A woman you may be in love with."

"I appreciated that; I let you take the lead there."

"I've spent half the night thinking this through and I don't want a divorce. A legal separation would take care of the estate and your will, assuming I'm still your primary beneficiary. Go have your fling…if that's what it develops into. I hope you live to see Tahiti."

"Thanks Irene…now let's call our attorney and get the legal wheels rolling."

* * * *

The days passed slowly for Helen, and each day she asked at the harbormaster's office regarding a message from Rodger. Each day there was none. Helen waited until almost noon on day three before entering the harbormaster's office. Diane, a pleasant woman Helen guessed to be about her own age, looked up from her desk. Pursing her lips, she gave a little shake of her head.

Sorry, Helen. Nothing yet." Helen's face must have registered her disappointment. Diane rose quickly from her desk and approached the counter. "I was just about to take my lunch break, Helen," she volunteered. "I hate to eat alone. Why don't you join me?"

"Thanks, I'd like that," pleasure registering in her tone of voice with anticipation of a possible friendship.

Once seated in the booth, Diane reached over and gave Helen's hand a reassuring squeeze. "Don't worry, Helen, you'll hear from your man."

A short laugh escaped Helen's lips. "You're very kind, Diane. But I'm not so sure I want to hear from him and…he's not my man." Diane's look of surprise prompted Helen to continue. "You see, he's married, Diane. He's gone home to divorce his wife…or not."

Helen found herself sharing their story, hers and Rodger's: his illness, his fantasy, and his hopes.

"His illness was messing up his life, taking away his life long dream, and robbing him of his place in his family. His solution was to leave it all behind, run away from home."

Helen paused as the waitress stopped at their table. Diane ordered a double cheeseburger with fries, Helen settled for a simple salad. "No wonder you stay trim," Diane scolded. "I feel obligated to my wardrobe to keep working at this plump figure of mine."

Once the waitress left them alone, Diane turned to Helen, her gray eyes serious. "I'm curious about something, though it may be none of my business."

Helen's steady gaze met her companion's inquisitive one. "I have no secrets."

"What made you volunteer to set off on a trip halfway around the world with a dying man?"

Helen was silent a moment, slowly stirring the dark liquid in her coffee cup. Finally, "I was so lonesome after my husband died. I couldn't get my life back together. There were no children who needed me. There seemed to be no purpose."

"I know the feeling, Helen. I felt the same way after my divorce, though I'm sure it's worse with a death. I sometimes wish we'd had children, my husband and I."

"Everything reminded me of Clyde, our house, and the furnishings. I lived in the memories of places we'd been, things we'd done. It took a year for me to bring myself to put the Sea Witch up for sale. Even then, I wasn't sure I could do it, we'd had such a good time aboard her. So when

Rodger shared his plans for a trip to Tahiti…well, it just seemed like a good idea. I could leave it all behind and still keep the Sea Witch."

Diane ran her fingers through her shoulder length, gray hair. "Sounds like you're running away yourself."

"Yes, I guess I am." Helen replied wistfully. "I just didn't think I'd learn to care for him so much."

"Imagine sailing off into the sunset with a dying man who suddenly has an attack of conscience and needs to resolve the problem by either dumping his wife or maybe aborting the trip."

"Diane! You make him sound heartless. I don't see Rodg that way at all. He's a nice guy, a nice guy with a dream and a serious health problem. He realized he couldn't leave his family that way. He returned to talk it out. Give him a break, Diane, he's trying to do the right thing by all people concerned."

Diane sat pensive for a while as she pushed her food around on her plate. "I just want this to be right for you, Helen. You're too nice a person to be disappointed by Rodger because of his marital problems."

"I appreciate your concern, but I've really enjoyed our voyage so far and the future could be very fulfilling for both of us.

"Ah ha! Cupid has entered the picture."

"Let's just say Rodger and I are very compatible." Having finished their lunch they both stood to leave when Diane suddenly walked around the table and embraced her. "I want the very best for you, girl."

When Diane and Helen returned to the office after lunch there was a phone message from Rodger. It said he would be arriving by seaplane tomorrow, and a decision had been made.

Helen turned to Diane, "I still don't have an answer, but I will tomorrow."

* * * *

The next day the daily seaplane made its spectacular, but noisy, approach to Port Angeles shooting a landing three hundred yards off shore and taxied in. Coasting to a stop alongside the floating dock for transient boaters, Helen stood waiting. Rodger, with a broad smile on his face, scrambled across the plane's pontoon and gingerly stepped aboard the floating dock. Taking Helen's hands in his he said, "Irene has set me free, so to speak, but does not want a divorce. She wants a legal separation and I have agreed. If we make it to Tahiti or I should say, when we make it to Tahiti, if I want a divorce, she won't fight me on it. He put his arms around Helen and hugged her tightly, as if he was embracing a new beginning for them. "Yes!" he repeated, "we're going to Tahiti."

Helen allowed her self to sink deeper into his embrace murmuring, "Thank God!"

Still hand-in-hand they walked to the finger pier where the Sea Witch rode easily at her moorings. The sun was warm as it passed its zenith. The wrinkled skin of the water gave hint of a slight summer breeze from the north. It looked ideal for an afternoon sail to their next landfall, Neah Bay.

Rodger led Helen aboard the Sea Witch and they embraced. Rodger then held her at arms length, "You won't believe how relieved I feel since I made this trip to Seattle. Irene and I have mutually filed for legal separation using the family lawyer. Irene came up with the idea; after some serious talk we realized neither of us needed this form of marriage any longer."

Rodger and Helen sat down on the cabin roof as Rodger brought her up to date. "We were staying together out of convenience and habit, neither of us living our lives as we wanted. We still care for each other and nothing changes as far as our estate is concerned. Irene will continue to live in our house; I'll live aboard the Sea Witch. We're both free to continue the rest of our life's journey as we individually choose."

"The big surprise to me is that Irene doesn't want to run the business, she wants our son, Junior, to run the business for us while she pursues a career in painting. Isn't it amazing that we both had fantasies, but she didn't talk about hers."

"Our sons say they will support our decision, even though it certainly wouldn't be their choice for us. I think they now realize I've stifled my dreams in order to be a good father and husband, but that's no longer necessary. Incidentally, Irene has never looked better, and she is looking forward to doing what she would have done after I died."

Helen turned and looked deep into Rodger's eyes, "I'm speechless, but happy. I told you I'd abide by your decision, but you know I so wanted us to be together in pursuit of your dream. You see, your dream has become my dream."

Rodger smiled lovingly at Helen as she continued. "Now, let's go ashore, have lunch and settle with the harbormaster. I'd like to say goodbye to Diane, she's been a real friend these past days. Helen glanced out across the bay, "If we can leave by one o'clock, we should make Neah Bay by six o'clock tonight, if that breeze out of the north continues to hold."

Rodger stood at attention and half-shouted, "Aye, Aye Captain."

* * * *

After lunch they settled with the Harbormaster, Helen and Diane embraced as they said their goodbyes. Diane, with tears in her eyes, watched Helen and Rodger board the Sea Witch, start the engine, cast off the lines, and slowly back out of the slip.

The breeze had stiffened enabling them to hoist the sails as they traversed the long run of Edez Hook. The Sea Witch, once again, was on its way to Tahiti.

* * * *

Chapter 6

▼

"With the wind and tide in our favor, the Sea Witch seems to be performing well." Rodger stated as they moved northward to their next port-of-call, Neah Bay.

"Right you are, Mate. At this rate we'll make Neah Bay about dinnertime, which makes me wonder why I use eating as a yardstick for travel? I guess this fresh air and good company makes for a robust appetite." Helen sat beside Rodger with the tiller between them.

"I wonder how the family is tonight?" Rodger said. "I wonder if they have gotten used to the idea that Irene and I will no longer be living together. It takes a little getting used to on my part too, as I've forgotten how it is to be single."

"Are you having second thoughts, Rodg?"

"Don't we always have second thoughts about the big decisions in life? I guess I just have to let the hand play out, at least for awhile."

"Well Rodg, anytime you think you've made a mistake, we can turn around. However, I suggest you do what you just said, let the hand play out for awhile."

"I guess you're right," replied Rodger. "However, I feel better having said what was on my mind. Now I can relax and just be here with you sailing to Tahiti on the 'Good Ship Sea Witch.' She is a good ship and I feel more comfortable about our trip each day; I'm feeling more comfortable with you, too. In fact, I'm not sure comfortable is a strong enough word for how I feel." Rodger looked ahead avoiding eye contact with Helen.

"Easy Rodg, I suggest we let that hand play out, too. Right now you are very vulnerable and I am too. This past year has been a roller coaster of emotion for me trying to learn to live without Clyde. I'm more comfortable with you, too, Rodg, so at least for now, let's concentrate on sailing this ship to the other side of the world and enjoy each day for what it is." Helen sat with the local navigational chart in her lap.

"Okay Helen, I hear you loud and clear; so what's the new compass setting, as here's the entrance to Neah Bay."

"That sneaked up on me. According to the chart it should be 240 degrees and about a mile to our night's moorage at the municipal marina."

Rodger stood in the bow as the bay opened up with the usual evergreen trees of Douglas Fir, Western Red Cedar, and Northern Hemlock, mixed with Madrona and Alder crowding down to the salt water shore. A portion of the bay's perimeter on the south side housed the Indian village of Neah Bay. Fishing is the source of its existence as masts of commercial trollers dominate the waterfront scene. Large drums on the stern of other boats indicate gill netting also shares a part of the fishing activity here. Smaller fishing boats, some commercial, some pleasure, occupy the rest of the slips in the marina.

The village, being the heart of the Makah Indian reservation, is a mixture of old and new buildings. A single road runs through the center of town and services the waterfront, disappearing into the forest at the far end of the bay leading to Tatoosh Peninsula. This being the very tip of the state of Washington, is bordered on one side by the Pacific Ocean, on the opposite side by Neah Bay, and faces the Straits of Juan de Fuca. Just off the tip of the peninsula, a distance of a few hundred yards, lays Tatoosh Island, its only inhabitant a lighthouse keeper. It is apparent Tatoosh Island was once a part of the peninsula. Time, with its erosion ability, has been at work here.

As the Sea Witch enters the bay, Rodger turns his attention to the marina. "They must have some pretty heavy weather here if they need a breakwater inside a bay this small."

"I think they do as we're less than a mile from the Pacific Ocean. There's a swale up ahead in those hills and I can imagine the wind really rips through there when there are storm conditions on the ocean." Rodger stood now at the tiller looking at the surrounding hills.

"I'm assuming that a swale is a valley or low spot," said Rodger. "That's what I'm seeing in that line of tree covered hills between us and the ocean."

"Right you are, Rodg. I keep forgetting that you're learning the language of a sailor."

They had motored into the marina after dropping their sails with Rodger at the helm. It was a successful landing and they were soon berthed for the night.

Helen finished tying the lines to the mooring cleats as Rodger flaked the sails. "Do you want to eat ashore or aboard?" she asked.

"Based on what you told me earlier, I opt for eating aboard. We have some lean hamburger; I could fix gourmet patties, a canned vegetable, and a salad. How does that sound?"

"Heavenly. While you cook I'll go ashore and buy charts for the West Coast and a Pacific Coast Pilot book. I've put this off until I knew for sure we were actually going."

"Very conservative of you; that surprises me."

"Well, we almost didn't go, remember? I guess it's just a part of my upbringing."

"Speaking of upbringing, where were you raised?" inquired Rodger finishing his sail tending.

"That's a long story; let's save it for dinner conversation, I want to get to the chandlery before they close. I hope they have the charts we need, at least for the first leg of this journey. We can buy charts later for the crossing."

Going below deck, Rodger gathered the makings of their dinner and placed them on the counter near the stove. While the stove was heating, he formed the hamburger into two large, thick patties after lacing them with chopped onions, garlic salt, pepper, and adding Worcestershire Sauce to the meat. As the meat cooked in its cast iron skillet, he sautéed onions to put on top of the patty. Contemplating their larder of canned goods, he chose canned corn as the vegetable, putting put it on the cooler part of the stove top to heat. He then turned his attention to the salad.

Deciding on a simple one of lettuce with sliced tomato, he spread them lightly with mayonnaise and paprika. After setting the table, he opened a bottle of Cabernet Sauvignon. Surveying his handiwork, he was pleased everything was coming together nicely when he heard and felt Helen step aboard. "Good timing, Skipper, dinner is just about ready. Did you find the charts we need?"

"I did, we now have charts to take us from here to San Diego," replied Helen. "That smells wonderful and am I ever hungry."

"Put the salads on the table, Helen, and I'll open the wine. I apologize for not having a Riesling for the salads, but this is the economy class cruise. Only one bottle of wine per dinner and the meat demands a Cabernet Sauvignon."

"I say it again. You are a find, Rodger. A real keeper, Rodger."

"You just keep thinking like that, Helen, and we'll get along just fine. Now, tell me about your family and your life growing up, that is if I'm not being too personal."

"No, Rodg, you aren't being too personal. After all, we are roommates, or should I say cabin mates," Helen quipped. "I was born in a little wheat-growing community in eastern Washington State called Jericho. It had a thriving population of about four hundred people, but the community was actually spread over an area ten miles wide and twenty miles long. You see, the ranchers had to have about 3000 acres to make a living, she explained. "Being high plateau country with no extra water for large-scale irrigation, the soil and water supply only allowed them to plant wheat every other year. On the alternate year the ground lay fallow, or they ran beef cattle on it."

"Did your family have a ranch?"

"No, my Dad was the superintendent of schools; he was a teacher before he became the elementary, junior high, and high school principal. Spending his entire career in Calico; he was a pillar of the community."

"What about your mother and your siblings, do you have brother's and sisters?"

"Mother was a stay-at-home Mom, for which I'm very thankful. I have two older brothers who treated me like a brother in my younger years; I fit into the tomboy role quite easily." Helen's green eyes twinkle as she warmed up to the subject and continued. "When I turned sixteen, they miraculously realized I was a girl. From then on they were overly protective. So much so that I wasn't asked out on dates often. It was like having three fathers waiting at the door. It took a very self-assured young man to run their gauntlet of questions and instructions."

Rodger exploded into laughter that unfortunately ended in a coughing, wheezing fit. "Sorry about that, but you do paint a vivid picture. No wonder you waited to marry."

Helen sat sipping her second glass of wine. "I decided to be a teacher like my father, and before I knew it I was so wrapped up in my teaching and my students that the years just got away from me. For some reason I never met Mr. Right until I was nearly fifty years old. As I told you, Clyde and I had ten great years together. Then, he had a heart attack and I was a widow. It was a year before I could bring myself to sell our boat, Sea Witch. I put an ad in the paper, and that's where you came in, Rodg."

Helen stood and started clearing the table. "You know Helen, I'm sure I would like your family. Are both of your parents still alive? They sound like salt-of-the-earth type people."

"Yes, Dad and Mom are enjoying retirement, still living in Jericho eight months of the year. They have a trailer they keep in a remote area in Baja, Mexico. It's a little place called Punta Chivata, where they spend December through March."

"How about your brothers?" Rodger, having finished his second glass of wine, helped with the dishes.

"They both married their childhood sweethearts, left Jericho, and each has two children. They live and work in the Seattle area." Helen turned and smiled at Rodger as talking about her family brought her pleasure.

"Thanks for the family run down. I can see why you're such a down-to-earth type of person, yourself." Rodger returned the smile feeling very relaxed from the good food and wine.

"Sometimes I wish I wasn't," blurted Helen. "Sometimes I want to kick over the traces and do crazy things: dress like a gypsy; sing, dance, maybe drink too much wine, find a man to run away with."

Rodger paused for a long moment. "Well, in a way, isn't that what you are doing?"

Helen's eyes widened in astonishment as she pondered Rodger's remark. "Do you suppose that's what I'm doing, being here alone with you on this adventure to Tahiti? If it is, I surely didn't know it when I offered to skipper the Sea Witch to Tahiti."

"Think about it, Gypsy." Rodger had an urge to grab Helen in an embrace and smother her with kisses, but thought it might be too much too soon. "I'm going topside and have my pipe while you finish the dishes."

Sitting on the cabin roof with his legs stretched out and feet on the gunnels, Rodger lit his pipe of tobacco with a kitchen match, and watched the flame temporarily light up a small portion of the immediate night sky. The simple act of blowing out the flame brought a series of coughing and wheezing, bringing him back to the reality of his health problem. *If only I wasn't staring death in the face, Helen and I could be Gypsies together. Come to think of it, what I'm doing isn't too far from what a Gypsy might do. I'm throwing caution to the wind, giving up all of the responsibilities that I have assumed over the years, running off with a fair maiden to an enchanted island. Sure sounds Gypsy-like to me.*

He gazed out across the bow where waves lapped against the hull. With a sigh of regret over a possible opportunity missed, Rodger knocked out the tobacco residue in his pipe against the gunnels and watched the still-live coals cascade into the inky black liquid of the bay. *The calm water, the soft gently warm wind, the night sky spilling over with stars, this is a night for lovers, or should I say Gypsies,* thought Rodger.

Rising to his feet, he descended down the stairs leading into the salon where Helen lay snuggled upon the divan, with a book in her hand. "I see you're settled in for he night, I was hoping we could play a game of cribbage or have a night cap or something."

"Well, I would enjoy a night cap, I'm not up for a game of cards. What do you offer for a nightcap?"

"I have a bottle of Drambui I've been saving for special occasions," ventured Rodger. "How about slipping on your jacket and we'll go topside to toast the stars. They're putting on quite a show tonight."

"Is this a special occasion, Rodger?"

"It could be," his voice reflecting his warming emotions.

"Rather than my jacket, I'll just slip this table cloth over my shoulders. Don't you think it has a sort-of Gypsy shawl look to it?"

"Now that you mention it, it does," replied Rodger as he stepped back to survey Helen from head to toe. "However the stripped, flannel pajamas under the shawl doesn't fit the gypsy picture, even though you do look fetching in them."

"Oops! I guess I have some shopping to do at our next port-of call." Helen giggled as she sprang lightly up the steps to the deck. "Oh how beautiful," she gasped, gazing at the star studded sky above them.

Rodger's gaze was fastened only upon Helen and the stars in her eyes. "Maybe it's time we picked up where we left off in Port Angeles," he whispered huskily.

"Where was that Rodger?" She said clutching the tablecloth shawl to her shoulders as she stood looking up at him playfully.

"You know, where we embraced when I returned from Seattle?"

"Oh, that!"

"Yes, that!" said Rodger with just a slight edge to his voice.

"Well, I guess we could embrace and see what happens."

They kissed and a wave of passion swept over both of them, blending their bodies into one. They clung to one another for a long moment, both feeling the warmth and pleasure of being wrapped in each other's arms. Suddenly Helen brushed her palms against Rodger's chest; stepping back one step, "Rodg, I think that's as far as I want to go tonight. This new relationship takes a little getting used to and I want it to be right for both of us."

"We both have some hurdles to get over," suggested Rodger, "but it's sure nice to be more than a friend." The tablecloth dropped to the deck as Helen slipped her arm around Rodger's neck; his arms slid about her waist. He lowered his face to hers placing another passionette kiss upon her lips.

"I agree, Rodg, we both have some hurdles to get over. Would you mind going below first? I want to stay up here by myself for a little while."

"I can do that, Helen."

* * * *

Chapter 7

Rodger was the first to awaken the next morning. Quietly dressing before pulling back the drape dividing his forward berth from the salon, he paused momentarily, watching Helen sleep. *She looks so childlike*, he thought, *curled up in her sleeping bag.* Rodger slipped into the bathroom, then making his way to the galley portion of the salon, put on the coffee. He's learned to strengthen it a little to accommodate Helen's taste, and one he's now acquired.

As the coffee starts to perk and the aroma permeate the salon, Helen slowly comes to life. She lies there for a moment looking at the ceiling trying to determine where she is. Recognition registers. Rolling over, she smiles whimsically at Rodger.

"Good morning; I tried not to disturb you."

"I like to awaken to the smell of fresh coffee brewing. That means someone else is already up, and I get to start the day with a cup of my favorite beverage."

"I must confess I was as much concerned about my needs as yours."

"Okay, spoil my princess illusion. While you fix breakfast, I'll go ashore, shower and continue my fantasy as best I can."

"Yep, I'm definitely creating a monster; however, a nice monster. What do you want for breakfast?"

"How about oatmeal and toast?"

"I can do that," replied Rodger. "I'll go topside while you put yourself together."

"Sounds like a plan."

Rodger checked the mooring lines. Finding everything shipshape, he took a sponge and wiped the morning dew off the flat surfaces of the boat. Hearing Helen moving about the galley area, he took that as a signal to return to the cabin.

Helen met him as she ascended the stairs. "Okay Mate, it's all yours; I'm off to the showers."

"Take your time. I'll put the oatmeal on and join you there. Well, not exactly join you, but…you know what I mean."

"Yes Rodg, I know what you mean. The tide change is in an hour and a half. I think we should try to cast off in an hour."

*   *   *   *

After breakfast Helen checked the chart and the weather report. It looked like another good sailing day ahead. They motored out of the marina as Rodger prepared the sails to be hoisted. Suddenly Helen shouted, "Hold up on the sails, Rodg."

"Why…aren't we sailing? There's enough wind!"

"Instead of sailing around Tatoosh Island we can take a short cut between the mainland and the peninsula side of the island. We need a full-slack to do that and we have it. We need to stay under power so we can follow a fairly straight route hugging close to the island's hundred-foot high granite face. Your job will be to go to the bow and watch for rock pinnacles that rise from the bottom. Tell me where they're located using the clock-face technique I taught you, and we'll be just fine as long as the weather holds with this three knot wind from the northwest."

"I'm glad you know what you're doing," called out Rodger looking ahead at their intended path. "It looks pretty dangerous to me with pinnacles showing all over the place between Tatoosh and the mainland. What caused them?"

"Tatoosh Island used to be a part of the Tatoosh Peninsula, and ocean waves and wind eroded the rock and soil over eons of time. The pinnacles are the parts of land and rock not yet eroded. The water close to the peninsula side of the island is deep enough to get through with a sailboat even with a four-foot draft, if you're careful and have a high, slack tide. However, if you are not careful, be prepared to swim."

"I see pinnacles barely below the surface of the water causing plumes of spray, sort of like little geysers," said Rodger.

"Those are not the problem. It's the ones deep enough not to cause little geysers, but less than four feet from the surface, that can tear the bottom out of your boat...but we save two hours by running this water gap."

"I can see this is going to be an interesting trip," replied Rodger grimacing playfully.

"You wanted an adventure, you've got it. Now go forward and be our lookout."

"Aye, aye, Captain. How far below the surface do these pinnacles have to be?"

"If you can see them under the water, they're too close."

Rodger scrambled forward and stood leaning over the bow sprite while holding on to the forestay behind him with one hand. "There's a pinnacle at eleven o'clock."

"Rodger!" acknowledged Helen.

"Pinnacle at twelve o'clock,"

"Rodger," replied Helen as she expertly guided the Sea Witch on its serpentine course. "Darn! The wind is picking up; that's not good."

"Do we turn around?"

"That's more dangerous than going straight ahead. Just keep looking for pinnacles, we're through the worst of it, I think. It's just harder to see the pinnacles with a chop on the water."

"Pinnacle at two o'clock."

"Rodger!"

"Should we be this close to Tatoosh Island, Captain? I can almost touch its granite face with my hand."

"That's the way it's got to be. That's where the deep water is. The granite face goes up a hundred feet and down twenty fathoms, I'm told."

"Great! Now, how far did you say a fathom was?"

"Six feet, so we're O.K., if our information is correct."

"Pinnacle at eleven o'clock."

"Rodger, Dodger, over and out!"

"What's this Rodger, Dodger over and out jazz?"

"That means the mission is over, we're home free. We're now in the Pacific Ocean."

"Phwee! This calls for a celebration. How about splitting an Old English 800 beer, even if it's early?" Rodger started to go below to the galley.

"Sounds good to me, but first let's hoist the sails so we can be sailing."

Helen pointed the Sea Witch into the wind. As Rodger hoists the main and mizzen sails, they begin luffing violently until Helen quickly lets the Sea Witch fall off the wind fifteen degrees. Once the sails fill, Rodger hoists the jib and they're on their way. The wind, being out of the northwest, comes across their aft quarter as they head south along the Washington coast. Rodger went below and returned with two glasses half-full of the robust, amber colored beer.

"I propose a toast," spoken as he hands Helen one of the glasses. "To the three of us. May our voyage continue to be successful and we see Tahiti."

"The three of us?" asked Helen as she stood beside the tiller guiding the Sea Witch southward.

"Yep, the three of us: you, the Sea Witch, and me. She has to be successful too."

"Agreed!" Helen held her glass up to Rodger's and looked deeply into his eyes. "To you and me and baby makes three."

For a long time they sat silently side-by-side in the cockpit sipping their drinks, savoring the actual beginning of their ocean voyage. The wind increased to fifteen knots and the Sea Witch picked up the rhythm of the rise and fall of the rollers. The air temperature remained in the high sixties, common for the Washington coast this time of the year. The sky was clear except for a bank of white clouds on the far horizon. It's the kind of day that makes mariners wonder why everyone doesn't follow the sailor's life.

"This is one big ocean, Helen," remarked Rodger as he stretched out on the bench seat of the cockpit.

"Seventy percent of the earth's surface is covered by water, Rodg."

"Really?"

"Jacques Cousteau has a lot to say about the ocean, he's that French scientist who has spent a lifetime studying it. According to Cousteau, it's a shocking paradox that at the precise moment in history when we're arriving at an understanding of the sea we should have to face the question, 'What if the oceans should die?' We've been ignorant and superstitious about the oceans and we're just beginning to learn how to manage and exploit this vast resource."

"This sounds like one of your lectures coming on, teacher."

"Yes, I guess it is. But think about it, if the oceans should die…it would be the final catastrophe in the story of man and the other animals and plants with whom we share this planet."

"That gets my attention. As I sit here and look out at the ocean, it looks so big and full of life. It's hard to imagine that it could become lifeless."

"It could happen according to Cousteau. If it did, the ocean would foul and become such a stench of decaying organic matter, it would drive people back from all the coastal regions in the world. That's just for openers. The ocean happens to be the earth's principal buffer, keeping balances intact between the different salts and gases our lives are composed of and which we depend upon."

"I get the picture, Captain. I have more respect for the ocean already and I'm sure there is more to this lecture, but you'll have to give it to me in small doses or my eyes glaze over."

"Okay Rodg, in the meantime, here's something else to think about. I think we need to add an autopilot to Sea Witch to make the trip more comfortable. Otherwise we'll have to stand four hour watches around the clock being constantly in control of the tiller."

"Around the clock watches sounds like a lot of work, and I'm for reducing work. Where'll we buy such a device along this primitive stretch of coastline?"

"I think Westport would be a logical place to have one installed. There should be a marina there with a ship's chandler near by and a mechanic to install it. Clyde was planning to have an autopilot installed when we took our trip to Tahiti. It certainly would make an easier trip for both of us. We'll be relieving each other at the helm and sleeping in shifts, as it is. But there would be a lot less strain on us while we tend the helm."

"By all means, let's pull in at Westport and have one installed."

"Good. I calculate Westport is thirty hours from here, so we'll get a taste of standing watch four hours on and four hours off during that run. If the wind holds we should get into Westport tomorrow-late afternoon. I'll stand the first watch, starting now, so you are elected to fix lunch."

"What would you like, soup or sandwich?" Rodger stood in preparation for going below.

"Both. Sailing always gives me a ferocious appetite."

"You could lose that schoolgirl figure, Helen."

"That hasn't been a problem in the past; just being aboard a moving, sometimes rolling vessel is a physical workout."

"I don't have any weight I can afford to lose. In fact, I hope to gain some weight and strength."

"I can already see that happening, Rodg. The physical workout of sailing, the three hearty meals we've been eating, plus all of the exposure to sun and wind, has been doing wonders on your appearance. In fact, I don't think you're coughing and wheezing like you were when we started this journey two weeks ago. Maybe this is just what the doctor ordered."

"Thanks for the kind words, Skipper. I hope you're right. On that happy note I'll head for the galley and fix lunch."

The wind remains constant as the Sea Witch takes on the characteristics of a colt set free from the corral, turned out on an endless prairie to run to its heart's content. This prairie of water is the Sea Witch's element. The constant swell and recession of the waves, waves that started as a water disturbance along the coast of China and worked its way to the coastline of the United States, causes the Sea Witch to take on a rhythm of movement that dips the bow into the nearest roller and the stern to lift on the last one.

The bow spray forms a soft rhythm of sound, adding to the ongoing symphony of the wind in the rigging, held taut like a violin string, by that same constant wind. The percussion section of this nautical orchestra is provided by the sounds emanating from the hull as it moves through the constant rising and receding of the waves. The reed and horn sections are the sails themselves, beating out a dramatic melody as the pulsing wind plays upon them. The conductor, standing tall at a tiller which substitutes for his or her baton, orchestrates this beautiful symphony with all the skill he or she possesses into one beautiful and dramatic masterpiece.

"Ahoy Mate! Where's that food? I'm starved!"

"It's coming right up, Captain," shouts Rodger as he sticks his head out of the hatchway. Expertly balancing food, he works his way aft. "Do you think this will do?"

"Yes Rodg, you are a find."

Rodger and Helen settle in the stern seat with the tiller between them. Helen controls the tiller with her left hand and holds her sandwich in her right. After Rodger finishes his cup of soup he takes the tiller so Helen can leisurely enjoy her clam chowder. The wind holds steady and the sun keeps the temperature in the high sixties. The tell-tales on the upper part of the mainsail tell Rodger they're trimmed just right for a broad reach. He slowly sips his coffee, aware of the rhythm of the Sea Witch; reminding Rodger of the rhythm of a carousel horse's steady, forward movement, lunging into the unknown.

"How long can we hold this tack?"

"Indefinitely, if the wind stays the same and our destination doesn't change."

"This is the life," says Rodger. "Is the trip living up to your expectations, Helen?"

"Yes, definitely!" Helen settled back into the cockpit. "You asked about my beginnings, how about yours? Where did you grow up and how did you get where you were when we met?"

Rodger settled back in the cockpit, "I grew up in a small town in western Washington called Silverdale; my dad worked in the nearby Puget Sound Naval Shipyard. Being a coppersmith, he plied his trade there for 33 years."

"A coppersmith," interrupted Helen. "What on earth does a coppersmith do in a shipyard?"

"A coppersmith is a plumber for ships and submarines. Navy ship's plumbing has been copper for a long time. It resists corrosion and bends easily to the many angles of a ship."

"Oh, I had him making jewelry or artistic things in copper."

"He did some of that, but only as a hobby. My mother was a stay-at-home mom, like yours. I have two sisters who have married and have children of their own. In fact, I am an uncle eight times over. Irene and I married after college where we met in our junior year. Both being business majors, we went to work in the banking business in Seattle. After five years I had learned the ropes in the mortgage business and, with the help of a venture capital group, started my own mortgage company. Irene joined me a year later after I determined we were probably going to be successful."

"That's pretty impressive. I know you have three sons and some grandchildren; how many grandchildren?"

"Seven by last count: four boys and three girls."

"It appears that you and Irene have done well and have had a full and successful life."

"Irene and I have had our share of bumps along the way. I thought after I retired I would finally learn to sail and take my voyage to Tahiti. Then with this unexpected health problem, suddenly time was running out. That's where you and the Sea Witch came in."

"I'm glad we did, Rodg."

✳   ✳   ✳   ✳

Chapter 8

▼

A combination of the late afternoon sun and steady wind provided a comfortable path for their journey southward. Helen sat at the tiller while Rodger stretched out on the cabin roof attempting a nap. At 3:00 o'clock Rodger took his turn at the helm as the Sea Witch continued southward through the gentle rollers. Small offshore islands dotting the coastline, showed no signs of habitation. Like tall wooden soldiers, the fir, alder and madrona trees marched down to the rocky beach that separated them from the ever present, crashing surf. Strewn on the upward edge of the rocky beach, twisted, bleached driftwood formed interesting and sometimes grotesque configurations.

Outcroppings of 200 feet high cliffs, backed by tall Douglas fir trees, interrupted long stretches of low-forested areas. Small islands, looking as if they had at one time been a part of the mainland, huddled off the rugged coastline. Again, there were no signs of habitation, only the never-ending ocean stretching to the south, north, and west.

"Helen, do you have the feeling we are the only ones on planet earth?"

"It does seem that way right now, doesn't it? We should be seeing some water traffic before too long since we're in the shipping lanes. I'm having second thoughts about making Westport our next port of call. La Push is only a few nautical miles ahead. We should make it there by late afternoon. I guess I'm not ready to sail at night along this coast with reefs like the Umatilla, the possibility of uncharted islands, the boat traffic; not to mention possible fog. We could go out beyond the shipping lanes, but I'm not ready for that either."

"Why Captain, do I sense some apprehension?"

"We'll soon be in unfamiliar water, and all of a sudden I'm thinking, wouldn't it be nice to have radar, a navigational system, along with our soon to be acquired auto pilot."

"If that's what we need, that's what we'll get. I want this journey to be a success. Would La Push have what we need?"

"No, it's just a fishing resort and Indian village at the mouth of the Quillayute river. La Push is the tribal village of the Quillayute Indian nation. I was here once with Clyde, but this is as far south as we ever sailed. As I remember it, there's a large haystack shaped, granite island just off shore. The main river channel snakes around the south side. The other side is non-navigable though there's water there. It's just never been dredged."

"I hope you remember which side is which." Rodger stood and scanned the coastline coming up. Ahead he spotted the haystack-shaped island.

"We have to go beyond the island, then do a buttonhook turn to pick up the channel entrance," explained Helen as she stood at the tiller. "A man-made jetty forms one side of the channel, and James Island's wash rocks formed the other side. The opening is about 40 yards wide, and if we stay in the middle of the channel with the engine at full throttle and the sails close-hauled, we should be able to overcome the current of the river. We'll also have the incoming surf to help push us shoreward at the most critical time."

"Really?" exclaimed Rodger. "This sounds almost too exciting."

"Remember! You said you wanted adventure, Rodg." Helen became silent as she looked over the pending entrance of a sailboat into a river mouth from the ocean. This would be a test of her nautical skills.

"Just tell me what you want me to do," said Rodger, "and when you want me to do it."

"Just before we get to the bottonhook turn, start the engine; then trim the sails so we're close-hauled. After you finish those two maneuvers, come back with me at the tiller and be ready for whatever I tell you to do. If everything goes right, there will be nothing to do except enjoy the ride."

"What could go wrong, Captain?"

"Well, we could have the engine quit and lose some of our ability to go forward. If that happens, slack off on the main and force the boom out in order to pick up as much wind in the sail as we can. If it will ease your mind, I'll go below and call the Coast Guard to be aware of us. There is a Coast Guard station right here within 300 yards of the jetty."

"I'd like that."

"Okay, I'll do it now." Helen moved across the cockpit to the companionway leading to the salon. A few minutes later she returned to the cockpit disappointment written on her face.

"What's wrong?"

"According to my radio contact, the Coast Guard station vacated La Push last year due to a lack of funds. The nearest station is either at Westport or Port Angeles."

"So much for that backup plan," said Rodger. "Why don't we just go south and be in Westport in the morning."

"I'm uncomfortable sailing at night without the equipment we need."

"Okay, sthen it's in we go. The engine hasn't been a problem so far," replied Rodger.

"I suggest you get two life jackets out of the locker; we might as well be prepared. It's standard procedure for situations like this. In fact, some sailors wear their life jackets all the time."

"I wouldn't like that; I'd just as soon keep them close at hand, if we need them."

"Our turning point is a hundred yards ahead, so start the engine now. As soon as we make the turn, trim the sails…I'll start our turn in three minutes."

"Aye, aye, Captain." Rodger quickly went below to start the engine and returned immediately to trim the sails.

"The engine sounds fine, sit with me and enjoy the ride," Helen called out excitedly.

"Hmm, I see what you mean about a narrow channel. With a four-foot keel, the middle of the channel has to be the only route we want. I hope those engineers did a good job of dredging when they created this entrance."

"Sea Witch has been in here once before; I'm hoping the river bottom hasn't changed since then."

"Those rocks in the jetty and the wash rocks are the size of Volkswagens; I'm guessing they wouldn't make for a soft landing."

"We're doing just fine," soothed Helen. "The Sea Witch is making about two knots against this current. See how the incoming surf lifts and pushes us through the entrance of the river? There's smoother water ahead and just around that dolphin ahead we'll hang a hard turn to starboard to the dock where the Coast Guard boats used to be moored. I'm assuming they didn't remove the dock, or gangplank."

"Whoa, I don't see a dolphin. A dolphin is a fish, right? And we're going to use it as a bearing to turn on?"

"Wrong! A dolphin is a cluster of three or more pilings driven into the ocean bottom by a pile driver, they're bound near the top with a steel cable to keep them together and strong."

"For what purpose?"

"They serve as a guide post for boats or an emergency bumper for boaters who can't make a sharp turn without being bumped partly around. All ferry boat docks have them. They also are used to display navigational markers."

Suddenly Helen's lesson was interrupted by a sputtering sound rising from below deck; then silence… "Damn…the engine died! Is this a self-fulfilling prophecy or what?" shouted Helen. "Go forward Rodg, slack off the main sheet…now! Force the boom out by sitting on the boom and using your legs as you walk backwards over the cabin roof and deck."

Jumping to his feet, Rodger released the main sheet, placed his bottom-side against the boom, and walked the boom out using the strength of his legs. Once they began to pick up more wind in the mainsail, they maintained their speed against the river current. Rodger dashed below deck in an attempt to restart the engine—and it caught.

Between the engine, the wind in the sails, and the incoming surf, the Sea Witch continued to overcome the power of the river current and move forward upstream.

"Hurrah!" shouted Rodger. "We're in smooth water, we must be beyond the river mouth and in the river itself."

"Right you are," a smile replaced the anxiety in Helen's face. "Now we can relax as the current isn't so strong. There's our starboard turn up ahead at the dolphin and voila, there's the deserted Coast Guard dock. I'm relieved that it's still here as it assures us safe moorage for the night. The only thing we'll have to contend with is the sound of the booming of the surf, being only a hundred yards away."

"I don't know about you, Helen," Rodger confessed, "but that was a heart-stopper back there for me when the engine quit."

"It was for me too. But at least we had a back-up plan and it worked. Maybe it was good training for us. Who knows, we may have more tight spots in the future."

Rodger dropped the jib, mizzen, and mainsail as Helen made the turn into the wind. "I see a lot of boat moorage up-river a short distance, but mostly empty. Where have they all gone? It's still the salmon season, isn't it?"

"The boats left when the salmon left. There's only a few thousand fish caught around here during a fishing season. Once upon a time several hundred thousand salmon were caught in the nearby ocean and brought here to the fish buyer's barges that lined the bank over there between us and the empty boat slips. It was a great set-up as the commercial fishing boats had safe moorage out of the ocean, and a place to sell their fish and get supplies."

"How come you know so much about salmon fishing, Helen?"

"Clyde tried his hand at it several summers, right here in La Push. That was before I knew him, but he told me all about it when we brought the Sea Witch here. I'll shift into neutral while you go forward and put out two bumpers on the starboard side. Then tie on a bow and stern line to the dock that's coming up.

"Aye, Aye Captain."

"I'll shift the engine to nuetral, so be ready to jump onto the dock and secure us."

"Aye, aye Captain."

The Sea Witch settled next to the dock and Rodger quickly tied the bow and stern line to appropriate dock cleats. He then established a spring line to limit the boat's motion fore and aft. After flaking the sails on the main and mizzen booms, he secured the jib with a bungee cord now lying in a neat heap at the bottom of the bow's forestay. Helen cut the engine and only the rhythmic booming of the surf permeated the air.

The village of La Push was strangely silent. Only an occasional bark of a dog gave any indication of habitation. The late afternoon sun was well on its way to disappearing behind the evergreen trees surrounding La Push on three sides. The Quillayute Needles, a line of jagged rocks extending an eighth of a mile into the ocean just south of James Island, dominated the rugged oceanfront scene.

"Where is everybody?" asked Rodger. "This is eerie."

Helen stated matter-of-factly, "The marina is a quarter mile upstream where the sport fisherman put their boats in the water. There's a store, cafe, and sleeping accommodations, if you're not too choosy. The tribe has relocated up the hill a mile in new manufactured houses nestled in the surrounding forest, which are far better than what they had down here near the beach. Those empty shacks are all that is left of the original village. There's only a store and motel on the road out to the main highway."

"I guess we really are at a jumping-off place."

"Let's take a walk before dinner and get the kinks out," suggested Helen. I'd like to walk the ocean beach once again. It's been awhile since I've done that. There is something mesmerizing about the rhythm of the waves. Some believe it induces a state of meditation."

"After that close call at the entrance to the river, I could use a little meditation. Is there someone here that could look at the engine to determine the problem?"

"I think I know what the problem is, based on the symptoms. Let me check the gas filter first. If it's clean, then we'll look for a mechanic. If it's dirty, that's probably the problem."

"Helen, you never cease to amaze me."

"Well, it all comes with the territory of being a skipper. We'll check it out in the morning; right now let's walk. I remember a path through the drift logs over there."

Sun bleached logs piled helter skelter atop one another lined the pebble beach. With the surf out exposing a hundred feet of beach, the waves came in straight, curled, and broke a hundred feet out, then feathered to make smaller breaking waves perhaps a half-dozen times before ending on the beach. The rocks on the beach, shone as if they had been dipped in lacquer. Muffled by distance, the first breaking waves created a soothing melody of their own.

"This is a beautiful spot, Helen. Let's walk down to the water's edge, I'd like to get a closer look at those ominous, needle-like rocks."

"Those are the Quillayute Needles named after this Indian Reservation of which La Push is a small part. They once were a part of the mainland, like Tatoosh Island where we ran the gap this morning. Wind and water have formed them. They're a danger to boats, especially if you're adrift. If you lose your power off the Needles, you'd better pray for an outgoing tide."

"You know, Helen, maybe the safest part of this trip will be when we're crossing the open ocean, not following the coastline."

"Time will tell, Rodg. Let's head back to the Sea Witch, I'm getting hungry. By the way, what's for dinner?"

"I was waiting for that question. How does boiled bratwurst sausage, sauerkraut, potatoes, sourdough bread, and a salad sound?"

"It sounds like heaven to me, Mate. Lead the way."

*   *   *   *

After dinner Rodger retreated to his favorite spot topside. There he could smoke his pipe and reflect on the day while Helen did the dishes. This day had had two exciting moments he decided: the running-of-the-gap off Tatoosh Island and sailing against the river current in the narrow opening to La Push when the engine faltered. He made a mental note to check the fuel line filter in the morning. If it just had residue in it, they'd have no need to seek the services of a marine mechanic, according to Helen. The easiest and best part of the day he concluded had been the six hours of sailing. The Sea Witch had become a living, breathing thing sending his senses soaring.

Rodger patted the bowl of his pipe into his open palm and let the ashes trickle into the dark obis of the water. Helen had just finished the dishes when he returned to the salon. "Did you enjoy your evening, alone-time?" he asked.

"Yes, although I never thought of it in those terms. I guess we do spend most of our time together, don't we? Don't get me wrong, I like being with you, but we do need to get off by our self daily to sort-of collect our thoughts."

"Do you do that when I'm cooking?" Rodger asked as he settled on the divan.

"Yes," replied Helen, "In fact I get three time-outs a day while you get only one, poor dear. I save all the dishes until after dinner to cut down on heating water. Besides, washing dishes is a chore I'm only willing to face once a day."

"Spoken like a true, dyed-in-the-wool pragmatist."

"A pragmatist? Yes, I guess I am. I've always felt that one should do whatever seems to work best."

"What do you say we turn in early tonight? I'm worn out after the excitement of the day."

"I'm with you, Mate!" exclaimed Helen, then breaking into a lusty laugh, "That is to say, I agree. I didn't mean I'm with you…like in bed."

"I know what you meant…although the idea has a certain allure to it."

"Good night Rodger."

"Good night Helen."

✳ ✳ ✳ ✳

CHAPTER 9
▼

The next morning Rodger checked the fuel filter and was overjoyed to find it had enough sediment in it to foul a carburetor. After carefully cleaning the glass bowl of the carburetor filter, he re-installed it.

Since Helen was still sleep, he decided to take a brisk walk along the beach instead of testing the engine. Inhaling deeply, he enjoyed the pungent, heady, iodine aroma of kelp, that lie off shore in shallow submerged beds. Spindrift, caused by the constant wind blowing across the open water and waves, gave the air an in-your-face salty smell.

When he returned to the Sea Witch, Helen was sitting topside, brushing her short, wavy, auburn hair. A pail sat beside her, socks and underwear soaking in warm water laced with salt-water soap. "Ahoy mate," she called as she spotted Rodger climbing through the tangle of beach logs nearby.

"Ahoy, Captain. Did you sleep well?"

"Like a baby. How about you?"

"My sleep was more like a 60 year-old baby with the croup."

"I'm surprised, I didn't hear you."

"You're a sound sleeper, Helen. It would have taken quite a bit to awaken you last night. The German's have a saying; *a clear conscience makes a good pillow.* You must have led a virtuous life."

"Yeah," Helen replied smiling, "up until now."

"Oh, ho!" chuckled Rodger, "Now that's a subject I'll look forward to discussing later. I checked the fuel filter, it was fouled as you suspected. I cleaned it so it's time to run the engine for awhile to determine if the problem is solved."

"The tide change is in an hour. I'd like for us to be on our way by then, if we don't need a mechanic," replied Helen as she moved to her bucket of soaking clothes.

"I'll start the engine, then put on the oatmeal; you can finish your laundry after I heat more water for you. In the meantime I recommend the beach walk; it is smashing, as we English are prone to say."

"Sounds like a plan, Rodg. I'll dump the water out of my washing bucket, and if you'll pour a teakettle of hot water in the bucket for rinsing, I'll be eternally grateful. You do understand, you do your own laundry."

"I wouldn't have it any other way," quipped Rodger as he moved to the cockpit area.

The engine caught right off and Rodger set the throttle at idle speed. As the cooking oatmeal rose and fell in a rhythm of its own in the double boiler, Rodger put on the coffee. Brushing off the stovetop with a potholder, he placed two slices of sourdough bread on the stovetop to toast; then he set the table.

Setting the oatmeal aside to thicken and cool, Rodger turned the toast. The coffee pot spewed its moist smell filling the salon with a pleasant and inviting aroma. When he heard Helen striding the length of the dock, he served up the oatmeal, toast, and coffee. Stepping back from the table, he draped a dishtowel carefully over his raised arm, waiter style.

Descending into the salon backwards, Helen turned and smiled to see the scene before her. "Where have you been all my life?"

"Eat your breakfast while it's hot; I'll shut off the engine and join you. Good news, by the way. The engine didn't sputter once, so we're home-free to head out after breakfast."

"Mmmm, this is good oatmeal. I do like stove top toast, and the coffee is skookum."

"Skookum, is that good or bad?"

"That means it's strong, or good. Or it could mean it's good and strong. The word comes from Chinook Jargon, the former universal language of the west coast Indian tribes. It was developed so they could trade with the Hudson Bay traders a couple of hundred years ago."

"Well then, eat up and we'll pray for a skookum wind for the day," replied Rodger, "but not too skookum."

* * * *

Rodger cast off the lines and jumped aboard as Helen started to back the Sea Witch away from the dock in a 180-degree turn to face the river. She then shifted from reverse to forward and the ketch slowly moved out of the back-eddy. Letting the current move the boat in a sideward motion until they were far enough into the river to turn to port, they now faced the ocean. Adeptly maneuvering the Sea Witch to starboard, Helen avoided the jetty rocks on the port side of the boat. The river current, with the help of the engine, moved them rapidly through the opening of the river and into the ocean.

A hundred yards off shore, the churning, choppy water of the entrance and surf dissippated to low rollers. Holding this westerly course for fifteen minutes, Helen took a new compass heading of one hundred and seventy degrees to stay a mile off shore. The wind held steady from the northwest, they maintained a starboard reach with sails trimmed taut. The tell-tells were parallel, as the hull speed reached a brisk six knots.

"Mate, would you take the tiller? I need to go below and dress a little warmer. Today is cooler than I thought."

"Aye, aye, Captain. Would you get my windbreaker while you're there?"

Rodger settled in beside the tiller feeling very much at home now with the Sea Witch. The wind buffeted his tanned face. Taking off his Greek fishermen's cap, he let the breeze play with his hair as he inspected the sweat line now staining his cap. Even his gray, turtle-neck shirt came close to fitting after a couple of washings and his dungarees didn't have that new look any more. The new beard was more gray than brown, which surprised him.

"Here's your windbreaker and a cup of hot coffee. Did I interrupt something?"

"As a matter of fact, you did. I'm getting older."

"Welcome to the club. I'd say that we're both well into the second half of our life's journey, Rodg."

"I think you are being generous. For you, perhaps, not me."

"Well, I may be too; life is full of surprises."

"As long as we're having this discussion, did you have a mid-life crisis, Helen? You know that period that sorta marks the transition between the first half of life's journey and the second half."

"As a matter of fact I did; we all do, you know. Mine came when I awoke in the middle of the night and asked myself, is this all there is? That's when my radar went to work and I met and married Clyde."

"You have radar? Tell me about that."

"I've discovered, when I really know what I want…information…opportunities…people somehow show up on my radar screen. It's like they were always there waiting to give me what I wanted or help me get it. However, because I didn't really know what I wanted…they didn't get through to me; they didn't get on my screen. We seem to have a filter system which blocks out unneeded information or stimuli. We really need this blocking device or we would probably go crazy, we're constantly being bombarded with stimuli or information. When we really know what we're looking for, the filter opens allowing what we need to get in."

"Interesting! Is that why, when I really knew that I wanted a sailboat to sail to Tahiti, everything fell into place? You had a boat to sell and then offered to skipper it for me because the need was there."

"Yes." Helen sat on the bench seat enjoying her role as teacher as Rodger continued to monitor the sea ahead of them.

"That's amazing!"

"It is, isn't it? That's why you have to be careful what you ask for, Rodg, because you'll probably get it."

"So you asked for a husband and you got Clyde."

"Yep, that's it in a nutshell. At a subconscious level, I always thought I would get married, but hadn't really pursued it. I let circumstance dictate my life up until my mid-life crisis, and then I knew I had to try to fulfill any unmet needs. I think that is what the mid-life crisis is all about."

"So you had an unmet need, put up your radar antenna, and in walked Clyde?"

"That's about the size of it."

"That's mind boggling." Rodger stood to relieve the stiffness he was feeling in his legs.

"You know Rodg, probably a lot of things that happen in life can be explained this way."

"You sound like a psychology professor."

"Now that you mention it, I do have a minor in psychology and once thought about going back for more training, if I got burned out teaching physical education. Fortunately, in teaching you get to use everything you ever learned at one time or another, so I didn't get burned out or bored."

"On that happy note," injected Rodger, "Would you like fresh coffee?"

"Yes, please. I'll take the helm."

"You've got it, Captain."

* * * *

The wind held steady from the northwest at ten knots as the Sea Witch moved rhythmically through the three-foot waves toward Westport, the next port-of-call. Seagulls followed hoping for a handout. With none forthcoming they soared off to other potential feeding grounds. The cloudbank on the far horizon promised a pleasant summer day with temperatures in the high sixties. Occasionally a seal popped out of the water with staring round eyes, their mottled gray-black coats shining brightly in the morning sun. They, too, were looking for a meal and soon tired of the present company when nothing was offered.

Rodger sat on the foredeck with his back to the mainmast drawing in deep breaths of tangy sea air. Unbuttoning his fading denim shirt to expose his lightly tanned skin to the morning sun, brought on an unexpected siege of coughing. Gaining control, he once again sat back taking in all that was going on about him. Occasionally, saltwater spray peeked above the gunnels, only to fall back to the sea. Seabirds soared overhead checking out the Sea Witch and its occupants. Satisfying themselves the Sea Witch belonged there; they would fall off in a sweeping chandelle turn, disappearing in the distance.

"Helen," called Rodger over his shoulder, "does it ever get any better than this?"

"No, Rodg. This is about as good as it gets."

"If it did, I couldn't stand it. Would you like me to take the helm again?"

"Oh…you want to conduct the orchestra?"

"Yes. It is like conducting an orchestra, isn't it?"

"Take the tiller while I go below to call the Coast Guard at Westport. I'd like to find out the best time to cross the bar." Helen stood and released the tiller to Rodger.

"Cross the bar? What are you talking about?"

"The bar, landlubber, is a submerged sandbank built up by the outflow of silt and sand at the mouth of any river, bay or harbor. In this case we're talking about Gray's Harbor into which five rivers flow: the Elk, John's, Chehalis, Hoquiam, and the Humptulips River."

"Wow! That's a mouthful, Humptulips."

"Yes, the native Indian names are a mouthful, but all a part of the beauty of the Northwest. It's important we cross the bar at slack tide in order to get the smallest wave action. Waves break when their height match the depth of the water beneath them, they start breaking when passing over the bar. They have been known to roll over big vessels in heavy weather when navigated at the wrong time of the tide and in adverse weather."

"By all means, call the Coast Guard."

Helen turned the tiller over to Rodger and disappeared below. After spending a few minutes on the two-way radio, Helen returned with a wry smile. "Guess what?"

"I'm afraid to ask." Rodger stood scanning the travel path before them.

"The Coast Guard informed me the best time would be between one-thirty and two-thirty this afternoon. We can't possibly make that tide change because Westport is fifty miles ahead. The next tide change is six hours later, but it will be close to sunset when we go over the bar and dark by the time we find moorage."

"What are our choices?" Rodger looked at Helen questioningly.

"We could stand-by out beyond the harbor, but it would be twelve hours before we have both daylight and slack tide. We would also have to stand four hour watches."

"I vote to go in at sunset and dock in the dark. At least we would be in a safe harbor for anchoring, even if we don't find moorage."

"I'm with you, Rodg. Besides, there will be a fair amount of illumination from the town of Westport and we'll have lighted channel buoys all the way. Once we find Westport, the marina should be well marked with lights. Just remember Red, Right, Returning."

"You've mentioned that before. What's that about?"

"When you're returning to a port or harbor or marina the entrance will be marked with a red marker or a red light on your starboard side, and a green light or marker on your port side. If that isn't what you see, you've missed the correct entrance. Stop immediately, or you could be on the beach. Back up until you can see both markers and be sure that the red marker is on your right as you are returning to a port. Thus the saying: Red, Right, Returning."

"I'm glad you know what we're doing."

"Evidently you never did any of your power boating at night, Rodg."

"Nope. I was strictly a day sailor. I always planned to take a course in navigation, but never got around to it."

"You were fortunate not running into trouble navigating around Puget Sound."

"I'll drink to that. Which reminds me, it's time I fixed lunch and I could sure use an Old English 800 about now."

"Do that Mate and I'll take the tiller."

Roger went below and surveyed the cupboard and icebox. *We're going to have to fill the larder before we leave Westport, plus top off the tanks with fresh drinking water. We'll probably need stove oil and diesel oil for the engine as well. With radar, G.P.I., and autopilot in our future, we'll be making port less often for supplies.*

Finishing his preparation, Rodger shouted out "Lunch is served," as he returned topside. "I thought we'd have a Mickey Mouse Special, chips, and our beer of choice."

"What's a Mickey Mouse Special? I know what our beer of choice is," replied Helen with a grin.

"Your culinary knowledge is really lacking, Skipper. A Mickey Mouse Special is a peanut butter and jam or jelly sandwich."

"Well, I do admit my shortcoming in the culinary field, but I am a very experienced eater and the sandwich sounds delicious. Don't forget, Red, Right, Returning."

"I'll probably never forget red, right, returning."

*   *   *   *

The hours sped by as the Sea Witch surged forward like a playful porpoise diving into the wind and the waves. The wind remained constant, as the sun passed its zenith on its journey to the horizon. Afternoon sailing conditions were ideal for a heavy-built sailboat like the Sea Witch. When Rodger took over the helm, Helen started looking for a comfortable place for a nap. Rodger, seeing what she was about, suggested "Why don't you stretch out in the cockpit, my lap makes a nice pillow."

"Well, that's good of you, Rodg. I do feel like a nap. It must be all this fresh air and warm sun." Helen stretched out on the cockpit bench-type seat, and after adjusting her position a few times to get comfortable, drifted off to sleep.

Twenty minutes later, upon opening her eyes, she discovered Rodger looking down at her. "Oh, that was a nice nap." Helen made no signs of moving. "I hope I didn't snore."

"Like a buzz saw."

"Really?"

"No, but you did have a rhythmic purr and I wiped the drool from your lips on several occasions. Other than that, you were quite charming in your slumber."

"Rodg, you are despicable." Still she made no move to sit up. "It's nice to lie here and watch the clouds drift by. I hope you don't mind."

"You don't get it, Helen. I love the closeness I feel to you at this moment. Now, if my legs hadn't gone to sleep, I would suggest you stay there longer."

Helen sat up slowly and murmured, "You really are despicable."

Rodger stood up straightening his legs, massaging them with his free hand. "You thought I was kidding. I would love to have you stay there forever."

"Forever, Rodg?"

"Well, at least until supper time. Speaking of supper, what do you want for supper?"

"We just had lunch, Mate. When the time comes, you can surprise me. In the meantime if you'd like to change positions, you can take a nap. Bedtime will be later than usual because of our late arrival in port."

"I can't think of anything I'd rather do."

Rodger curled up on the bench-seat of the cockpit and lay his head gently on Helen's lap. Lying there watching the waves trying to creep over the gunnels, he drifted off into a light sleep.

Helen smiled as she looked down at Rodger. *His gaunt look is all but gone with the daily exposure to the sun and wind. He's putting on weight, so he must be thriving on his own cooking. He still has that terrible cough, but he doesn't seem to cough so often now.*

After a few minutes Rodger opened his eyes. "Have I been asleep?"

"Yes, Rodg, but only for about five minutes. Go back to sleep."

"That's easy for you to say," he mumbled, but immediately fell into a deeper sleep. When he awakened he was still looking at the top of the waves at the nearby gunnels. "You know, Helen, I had the strangest dream about waves; I mean big waves."

"Well, they have them here on rare occasions; they call them Tsunami waves."

"Oh yes, I've heard of them. How big do they get?" Rodger sat up to have eye contact with Helen.

"Bigger than you'll ever want to see. I've heard of them being seventy to a hundred feet high." Helen scanned forward in search of potential obstacles; all was clear.

"Wow! That is bigger than I want to see. What causes them?"

"Underwater movement of the earth's crust or volcanic eruptions," replied Helen as she moved to a standing position with the tiller encased under her arm.

"No kidding? I do know they have earthquakes up and down the Pacific Coast, but I hadn't thought about the resulting wave action." Rodger sat back wih his hands entwined behind his head giving Helen all of his attention.

"There are two earth crust plates that come together about fifty miles off shore from where we are, called the Pacific Plate and the San Juan de Fuca Plate. When they move, they disturb the water action and can cause a Tsunami wave. Also an earthquake as far away as Alaska or Japan can cause a Tsunami right here on this coast."

"Really? Are they just one big wave or are they a series of waves?" asked Rodger fully engrossed in the subject.

"Usually there is a series of waves and they move rapidly, but run out of water soon. Even people on land head for high ground when they get word of a Tsunami headed their way."

"I'd hate to be in a boat and have one coming at me. What would you do, Helen?"

"Put the boat's stern to the wave, if there was time, and pray. There are rogue waves occasionally, but they're not as dangerous as a Tsunami. Waves have a pattern of seven; the seventh being larger than the preceding six waves. Sometimes that seventh wave can be twice as big as the preceding waves, for whatever reason. It's called a rogue wave and can be dangerous."

"On that happy note, I'm going to retreat to the safety of the galley and start dinner."

"Just stay where you are, Rodg. It's too early to start dinner; lie back down. I like the feel of your head in my lap, too."

"Well, we can get even closer, if you are a mind to," said Rodger with a twinkle in his eye.

"No...Rodg...but after being alone for a year it's nice just to touch, to be near, just to talk. Do you know what I mean?" Helen's voice was soft with emotion.

"Yes, Helen, I do. Even though Irene and were married, there was a distance between us. I felt lonely a lot of the time, which was probably as much my fault as hers."

"You know, Rodg; I think you and Clyde would have liked each other; I know he would have liked you."

"That's a nice compliment, Helen. There is one thing he and I have in common."

"Oh? What's that?"

"You."

* * * *

Chapter 10

▼

The sun hung momentarily suspended on the far horizon as the Sea Witch approached the mouth of Gray's Harbor. Lights were coming on around the perimeter of the bay. Up ahead the water was lumping up and a wave line was apparent. The beach scene had changed from rugged cliffs to long sandy stretches interrupted by an occasional Indian village like Taholah or a seaside town like Moclips. Over fifty miles had been virgin timber, being a part of the Olympic National Park. But now it was low sandy beaches backed up by berms, marshes and tanglewood until foothills stopped the oceans dominance.

"That's the bar up ahead, Rodg. It'll be choppy for a short while, but nothing we can't handle. We'll be going with the waves so it should feel like a surfboard ride. Ever ride a surfboard?"

"Yes, I have...I'm going to like this."

"Good! If I thought this was dangerous I'd have us put on our life jackets. On second thought, that might not be such a bad idea."

"Somehow I'm getting a mixed message, Captain."

"Just hand me my life jacket without an analysis and keep your eye out for drift logs. You never know what to expect in these harbor areas."

"I see the red marker, Captain, it's on our starboard and the wave line is coming up fast."

"Hold on, Rodg...here we go."

"You're right," Rodger whooped. "This is like riding a surf board. I can feel the waves grab us amidships just like they used to grabbing me at the waist when I was a body surfer in southern California." Rodger stood to better watch the line of the waves they were in.

"I didn't know you were a body surfer, Rodg. I'll bet that was fun," exclaimed Helen thrilling to the excitement of the ride.

"It was more fun than board surfing." Rodger continued to look out to the wave line the Sea Witch was in, that extended on each side of the boat. "You became the surfboard, just like the Sea Witch is the surfboard on this wave at this moment"

"I see what you mean," said Helen letting her eyes travel the wave line as Rodger had. "I do feel like we're the surfboard and look at that bow wake. Unfortunately, the wave action ahead is petering out, so I guess our ride is about over."

"That was fun! Now, I guess we need to find Westport," said Rodger as he scanned the coastline of the bay before them. It was that moment of time between day and night called twilight when images become distorted and waiting shadows tend to dominate.

"With these long, northwest twilights, finding the marina shouldn't be a problem." Joining Rodger in the coastal search for their destination, Helen let her eyes scan mostly to starboard. "See how the bay has opened to become many times wider than its entrance," exclaimed Helen as she let her free arm point out the immensity of the bay. "There it is! The lights to starboard belong to Westport. When we get closer we should be able to pick out the marina and its entrance," she continued. "If our approach is correct, the red marker will be on our starboard side. Red, Right, Returning."

"I get the picture, Captain, but shouldn't we have our running lights on?" asked Rodger with an 'I gotcha' look in his eyes.

"Yipes! I was so hung up on surfing and navigating I forgot them. Thanks for the reminder. Go forward and check the bow lights. It's hard to tell from here in this twilight if they're on."

"The green and red bow lights are on," called out Rodger as he moved forward to the bow. "The white running light on the top of the mast is also on. We're in good shape."

"There aren't many boats out this time of evening, most people seek a snug harbor long before nightfall. Keep your eye out for the marina entrance and we'll find our snug harbor too."

Rodger moved back to the cockpit beside Helen. "There it is, dead ahead. Good navigating Skipper." Rodger now stood on the gunnels to starboard as he scanned ahead holding on to mainmast shroud. "I can see the red light; if you'll veer a little to port, that'll put it on our right side. Red, Right, Returning; I haven't been there, but I am returning, right?"

"Let's not overdo it Mate," chuckled Helen as she stood letting her gaze join Rodger's. "It's time to go in on the engine. As I turn into the wind, go forward and drop the jib, mizzen and mainsail; then flake and tie them so they'll be out of the way. Also get ready three bumpers and three mooring lines for docking."

"Aye, Aye, Captain."

"Also keep an eye out for the harbormaster's office; the transient dock should be near it. I hope they have a slip for us, I'd prefer not to anchor out."

"There it is to starboard, Captain. Over there by the gas dock." Rodger stood pointing to port with three bumpers in hand.

"I see it! Tie the bumpers on the port side and tie a bow and stern line for us. I'll shift to neutral and we can glide in. Grab the boat hook and be ready to snag a deck cleat on that dock coming up." Helen strained to see as the docking distance shortened. "I'll give the engine a little reverse power to slow our glide. Be ready!"

Rodger leaned over the rail with the boat hook in hand, snagged the upcoming deck cleat and brought the Sea Witch to a complete stop. Jumping onto the dock, he tied the stern line loosely, then the bow line. Readjusting both lines, he tied a spring line. They were now able to leave the boat to register for the night with the harbormaster.

A tall, angular man looking as if he had just stepped off the label of an 'Old Spice After Shave' bottle assigned them a slip for the night and collected the mooring fee of fifteen dollars. This also included a simple map of the facilities, with their appointed slip circled in red, and a handout pertaining to the marina rules.

Returning to the Sea Witch, they started the engine, untied the lines, and with Rodger in the bow acting as a lookout, made their way to the assigned slip. After securing the boat for the night, they grabbed their towels and toilet kits and headed for the marina showers.

"Two days without a shower takes some getting used to," said Rodger as they walked along the floating walkway. "There seems to be a fair number of pleasure boats here, but not the commercial fleet it once had."

"How do you know that?"

"I was here once for sport fishing. That's when salmon were plentiful. These slips were mostly full of charter boats, and this was a very busy place. Today it looks like it's operating at half capacity. Here's the shower area; I'll meet you at the Sea Witch afterwards."

"O.K., but take your time. I plan to have a long, hot, steamy shower."

"Sounds like heaven," replied Rodger, as he walked into the men's part of the facility.

* * * *

Rodger was in the galley fixing dinner when Helen stepped back aboard. Her hair wrapped in a towel, she wore clean denims, and a long sleeve polo shirt. Rodger had changed too, but he'd changed something else that brought a gasp from Helen. "Rodger, you've shaved off your beard."

"What do you think?" He stood back for her to get the full effect of his changed appearance.

"Why, I think it makes you look ten years younger...I wish I could erase ten years that easily."

"I'll take that as a compliment. I've tried to grow a beard before, but I've come to the conclusion that some men are just born to shave, and I'm one of them. I couldn't stand that scruffy looking, itchy beard any longer."

"I do like the mustache, Rodg."

Rodger's eyes twinkled, an impish smile tugged at his lips, "George Bernard Shaw, the playwright and author, said 'kissing a man without a mustache is like eating your food without salt and pepper.' Come here and see if you agree."

Helen didn't move, but her face lit up with pleasure. "What brought this on?"

"I guess a woman fresh out of a shower, her hair tied up in a towel turns me on."

"How could a woman resist an invitation like that?" Helen now moved over to the galley side of the salon and stood beside Rodger. He turned, smiled, took her in his arms, and kissed her tenderly and long.

"George Bernard Shaw was right," replied Helen. "There is something special about a kiss from a gentleman with a mustache. By all means Rodger, don't shave it off."

"Why don't we celebrate tonight. Let's have supper at one of those restaurants I saw across from the marina."

"What are we celebrating, Rodger?" Helen asked coquettishly.

"Maybe we can figure that out later," Rodger replied all smiles.

Rodger put away the start of his dinner preparation while Helen dried and brushed her hair. Each grabbing a light jacket they walked up the steep gangplank to the street level of Westport. The main street looked to be four blocks long with all of the businesses on one side of the street, the water with the marina on the other side, but at a lower level. This gave every business a view, as Westport sat high above the bay. The businesses looked right over the top of the marina.

Neon signs lit up the night sky and the sidewalks were crowded with happy vacationers. Businesses seemed to have struck a deal as to their locations along the street. There would be a restaurant; a gift shop, a charter boat office, and a dress shop featuring nautical wear. This sequence was repeated over and over again. The jovial crowd carried Helen and Rodger along until they came to a restaurant sign that stopped them in their tracks. The sign read 'Sea Witch' restaurant.

"How could we not eat here?" asked Rodger.

"I agree." Taking his arm Helen tugged him through the door. "It looks like they have room for us."

The proprietor, a short man with a happy smile, greeted them, and then led them to a table by the window. The furniture had a patina from many years of use, as did the floor and walls. The décor was definitely nautical and a sultry looking woman's face and upper torso had been painted on the main wall of the dining room, draped fishing nets provided a border. Her long, tousled, sea-weed-like hair hung over bare shoulders and bust ending at her waist. She had an inviting, but sinister half-smile on her pale, brooding face. Her arms stretched out, as if to embrace or perhaps strangle.

"There's the Sea Witch, Helen, but I prefer our Sea Witch."

"I do too. But enough of this small talk, let's eat. I'm starved."

"One thing about you, Helen, you are consistent."

"First things first, Rodger, old boy. First I satisfy the beast within and then I can concentrate on other things." Helen then buried herself in her menu.

"Like what?" asked Rodger not willing to drop the subject.

"Like whatever it is we are celebrating. What is it we are celebrating, Rodg?" She put the menu down, sat back and waited for an answer.

"Well, we can be celebrating the fact that we're not eating my cooking. Or we could be celebrating our safe arrival at Westport, or we could be celebrating that kiss. Take your choice."

"I like your cooking, the fact that we arrived safely today is no big deal, because we had no major obstacles to overcome. I guess that leaves the kiss." Her face grew serious as her eyes fastened on Rodg's face. "It was a very nice kiss; what does it mean?"

"It means I want to be more than friends, Helen. It means I want what you want, whatever that is."

"Well, let's leave it there for the time being as this takes some serious thinking." She looked away breaking their gaze. "In the meantime let's enjoy each day on our trip to Tahiti. Tomorrow we'll find a chandler and see about buying the accessories we need."

The waiter interrupted them. Quickly they stopped their conversation to peruse the menu. When he returned they ordered steaks and a bottle of Cabernet Sauvignon.

"A chandlery is one type of store I didn't see on Main street. But there has to be at least one in a seaside town like Westport," continued Rodger. "I noticed sailboats like ours with the rudder connected outside the transom had a weathervane type of apparatus for auto-steering. Is that what you had in mind, Helen?"

"It could be. I want to talk to a boat mechanic first. Buying these things is one thing, we have to hire someone to install them, unless you are a mechanic."

"If I knew how to install radar, radio, and autopilot, you'd be the first to know. As it is, I am not a handy man, I'm in the mortgage business, or at least I was. Ahhh, here's the wine."

The steaks were excellent as was the rest of the meal. They finished the bottle of wine and lingered over coffee. Deciding to have a nightcap aboard instead of dessert, they walked back to the Sea Witch arm-in-arm, enjoying the night air. As they approached the step over the gunnels to the deck, Rodger stepped ahead and extended his hand to lead Helen aboard. He then preceeded her down the companionway and stood at the bottom with arms extended. Helen walked into his arms and they kissed long and passionately.

"What do you have in mind, Rodger?" Helen asked knowing the answer.

"I think it's time for us to be lovers. Do you want to be lovers, Helen?"

"Yes, Rodger, I do."

* * * *

CHAPTER 11

▼

The sun streaming through the salon window awakened Helen. She snuggled into the sleeping bag reluctant to release the warm memories of the night before. She closed her eyes listening to the morning sounds: the lapping of the waves against the hull; the roar of a boat's engine coming to life on the far side of the marina; and the sound of high-heeled shoes clicking down the dock making a discordant sound in the disrupted morning wakeup serenade of the marina. Helen thought, b*oat people don't wear high-heeled shoes. They wear soft-soled shoes to protect their boats and to avoid a possible fall overboard.* The hard-soled shoes have stopped outside the Sea Witch, there's a knocking sound on the side of the hull.

"Anyone home?" asked a feminine voice.

"Yes," Helen answered. "Just a minute." Pulling on her yesterday's clothes, she worked her way up to the deck. A young, well-dressed woman in a business suit complete with briefcase stood alongside the Sea Witch.

"What can I do for you?" Helen inquired openly eyeing the woman up and down.

"Is there a Rodger McCauley aboard this vessel?"

"Yes, but he's sleeping. We were up pretty late last night."

"May I see him? It's important I do." The young woman stood resolutely.

"I'd ask you aboard, but he'll not be ready for company. Helen cast a meaningful glance toward the woman's feet. Besides, high-heeled shoes don't belong on a boat. Wait here and I'll get him."

Helen disappeared into the salon and made her way to the forward v-berth area. "Rodg, you've got company."

Rodger rolled up on one elbow and stared sleepily at Helen. "What? Who wants to see me? Who would know I'm here?

"I have no idea, but she's pretty and she asked for you by name. Have you not been telling me everything, Rodg?"

Rodger quickly pulled on his clothes, patted his rumpled hair a couple of times as he crossed the salon to the stairway. He stumbled up the stairs, his mind still groggy with sleep *who nows I am on the Sea Witch, in Westport, and has business with me?*

"I'm Rodger McCauly. You want to see me?"

The young woman stepped closer and reaching across the gunnels handed Rodger an envelope.

Opening it Rodger stared at the paper now in his hand. "What's this? A subpoena? Is this about the legal separation?"

"I'm a process server and your wife wants to see you in court. I've done my job, so goodbye Mr. McCauly." She turned to walk away.

"Wait! How did you know we'd be here in Westport and at this time?"

"Simple. I asked the marina to notify me when you hit port. This was the only logical place for you to stop along the Washington coast. Does that answer your question?"

"I guess so. What happens now?"

"Read your subpoena, Mr. McCauley." She turned, her high heels clicking on the wooden dock, as she retraced her steps.

"Well!" said Helen. "This is a surprise. What does the subpoena say?"

Rodger sat down on the cabin roof of the Sea Witch and slowly worked his way down the page. "I have a court date for September 5th in Seattle at the courthouse at nine o'clock with a Judge Long. Today is the second of September, so I have two days to get back to Seattle. What does she want that we haven't already talked about and settled?"

"Well, there is just one way to find out. If you don't show up, she gets it, what ever it is."

"I guess you're right. Do you want to go with me?"

"No, this is your affair Rodg. I couldn't be of any help to you. I'll stay here and get the accessories we want installed on the Sea Witch. I'll have plenty to do while you're gone."

"Damn, this is a nuisance. Rodger slapped the paper against his thigh. I can't imagine what this is about. Maybe I should call Irene and find out what the problem is."

"Suit yourself, but it probably won't effect the court date."

"If I call, at least I'll have an idea of what I'm walking into."

"Let's start the rest of the day off right. Go shower, put on your traveling clothes, and I'll cook us some breakfast."

"Okay. I'll check the bus schedule while I'm at the harbormaster's building and then make my call to Irene. Maybe the trip can be avoided."

"O.K. Rodg, but just know you have power; don't let her run over you."

"I hear you. I'll be gone a half hour at least so don't rush breakfast."

Rodger collected his clean clothes, towel, toilet kit, and walked to the harbormaster's office. The marina was coming to life, seamen and vacationers were beginning to fill the sidewalks and dock area of Westport. Rodger found a bus schedule posted on the bulletin board near the shower area. *A bus departs at 10.00 o'clock a.m. and arrives in Seattle at 3:00 o'clock p.m. after a transfer in Olympia. That'll give me a day in Seattle before the court date.*

Showering and completing his morning ritual, Rodger dressed in kaki pants, polo shirt, loafers and windbreaker-type jacket. Studying himself in the mirror, he was surprised at his reflection. Looking back at him was a man, tan from the sun and fuller in the face than he remembered himself being. *This is the new me. The shadows are gone from under my eyes and I look more alive. I'm not coughing as much, and even when I do, it's less painful. Life on the Sea Witch and life with Helen is definitely agreeing with me.*

Rodger located a phone outside the shower area and dialed the familiar number of his home. He listened. Pictured the room as the phone rang. *"Is this still my home? he wondered. Is this still a part of my life?"*

"Hello.

"Hello, Irene; this is Rodger."

Hesitantly the voice on the other end of the line answered, "Where are you?"

"I'm in Westport. I was served a subpoena this morning by your process server and I want to know what's going on?"

"Our attorney wants us to go to court before you leave the continental United States and get our property settlement legalized. He also wants the judge to be able to ask you the traditional questions before he can grant us a legal separation, I realized you won't be available at the end of the ninety day waiting period. This won't change the time-line on the legal separation, if that's what we still want."

"Are you having some second thoughts, Irene?"

"Well, let's at least hear what the judge has to say."

"I'll arrive at the bus station this afternoon at three o'clock if you want to pick me up. Otherwise, I'll take a taxi home. It is still half my house, so I guess I can call it home."

"Yes, it's still your home and mine. Either Junior or I will pick you up at the bus station at three."

"It'll be good to see the family." Rodger hung up and walked slowly back to the Sea Witch. He thought about the phone conversation and wondered if Irene had told him everything that was on her mind. *It seemed straight forward enough and logical, but on the other hand she went to a lot of trouble to stop me on my journey. Well, I'll know soon enough.*

After breakfast aboard the Sea Witch, Helen walked him to the bus stop. Taking in the sights and sounds of Westport, they made their way through the vacation crowd and those that served them. As the bus pulled up, Helen kissed Rodger lightly on the mouth, then stepped back to watch his departure.

"I should be back in four days; I'll leave a message for you at the Harbor Master's office if there is a change in plan."

* * * *

Helen slowly made her way back through the crowd of people. As her mind sorted through the arrangements she needed to tend to before Rodger's return, she noticed a group of four Hispanic looking seamen working with stacks of crab pots. Stacking the pots one on the other in long rows, they had about a hundred pots ready to be used. Helen approached the oldest member of the group not knowing whether she should speak in English or her poorly spoken Spanish, she decided on English. "Excuse me, is there a ship's chandler in Westport?" Much to her surprise, the oldest man wasn't the one who answered. A younger man with a noticeably Spanish accent chose to be the spokesperson for this group.

"What is that, Senora?"

"Is there a ship's chandler in Westport?"

"What is that, senora? A ship's chandler, I never heard of—"

"A place that sells parts and supplies for boats," interrupted Helen.

"Oh, Yes, senora. There is such a store, one block beyond Main Street that sells to us the things we need for our boats. It's called Westport Marine Supply."

"How do I get there?"

Pointing he said, "Go one block beyond Main street, turn left, and it's a couple of blocks down on the right side of the street. If you come to the Coast Guard Headquarters, you've gone too far."

The four men paused in their stacking, entranced with this woman who wanted to do business where they did business. "What did you call that again Senora?" the young man asked.

Helen laughed. "A chandler, and thank you for your help." She crossed the street following his directions. She was amused at the names of restaurants, stores, motels, and hotels she passed. Whale was used more than any other nautical word. The Hungry Whale a restaurant on her right, opposite a charter business by the name Whales Are Us, was beside a hotel called Orca Inn. *Yes,* thought Helen, *salmon is no longer king around here.*

Arriving at a one story, flat-roofed building with a small sign that read Westport Marine Supply Co., she opened the door. A young, male clerk turned, started toward her; then abruptly turned and walked away. M*ale chauvinist,* she thought. The tall stacks of marine supplies overwhelmed Helen. There didn't seem to be any order to things. She approached the only employee in sight, a middle-aged woman manning the cash register.

The woman's haircut, and clothes were those of a man, but she also wore jewelry and cosmetics. Taking a long drag on her cigarette slowly letting the smoke roll out before she spoke, "What are you looking for, Honey?"

The affrontry of the greeting lifted the hairs on the nape of Helen's neck. Regaining her composure she forced herself to calmly reply, "I'm looking for a G.P.S. navigation system, a radar system, and a weather-vane type auto pilot to be installed on a thirty foot sailboat. Do you sell these?"

"Are you the skipper?"

"Yes! Do you have these things?"

"Well," drawled the cashier, "we have catalogues and we can order it for you, we're just a branch store here. The main store is in Astoria, Oregon, but we can get it here by auto freight in two days."

"Is this the only chandlery in town?"

"We're it, Honey."

Helen felt the hair moving again on the back of her neck. "Do you install what you sell?" she asked bruskly.

"No, but John Day does; he lives in South Bend."

"I hope that's not the South Bend in Indiana," replied Helen trying to keep the sarcasm that she was feeling out of her voice.

"No, our South Bend is 45 miles from here and John's on call. I'll give you his phone number, if you'd like. You can find out what his workload is before you order your systems. He does good work and his per hour rate is reasonable."

I'll just go with the flow, resolved Helen. "What's his number?"

"It's 360-465-8321. If you have a phone calling card you can use my phone."

"I don't have a calling card, but I could ask the operator for charges and pay you. I'm going to be out of the country and won't be receiving or paying any bills for a while. Why don't you call your wholesaler first and see if they have what I want before I make arrangements for someone to install it?"

"Sounds like a plan, Honey." Helen struggled to control her impatience as the cashier placed her call…then chated amicallly with the clerk on the other end of the line. Finally replacing the phone the cashier turned back to Helen, "they've got what you need, Honey. It'll be here in two days."

Helen placed her call to John Day. He promised to make himself available when the systems came in. "In fact," he added, "I'll be in Westport tomorrow on a small job and I'll stop by the Sea Witch and scope out the job as I'm not familiar with a Tahiti Ketch."

Helen gave him the dock and slip number, "I'll try to be aboard when you arrive, if you can make it around noon." Helen then turned her attention to the catalogue. With a sigh of relief, she handed the cashier the check Rodger had pre-signed and given her.

"I thought you said you were the skipper? This isn't your check," the cashier stated bluntly.

"I am the skipper, but not the owner of the boat. If this is a problem, call his bank and I'll pay for the call."

"Sounds like a plan, Honey." Helen fought back the indignation threatening to capsize her self-control. The cashier placed the call, satisfied she faced Helen again. "Where's your boat, Honey? We can have it delivered there, if you like."

"No, have it delivered here; I'll call or stop back to see if it's in. John will be here to install it in three days."

"See you later, Honey, or should I say Skipper?"

"Do me a favor; since I'm not your honey, or ever will be, just call me Skipper." Helen, having made her point with the cashier, resisting an urge to slam the door behind her, strode out of the marine supply building to walk the two blocks back to the center of town.

* * * *

As she strolled towards town, Helen noticed for the first time, an observation tower at the end of the street rising above the buildings and the sea wall. It was obvious this sea wall kept the Pacific Ocean out of the streets of Westport. She decided to go the extra two blocks to the tower in order to get a better lay of the land. Upon reaching the bottom of the tower, her attention was drawn to a derilect old man seated by its base. In front of him was an array of clam shells split in half with various sailing ships outlined on them in India ink.

With a polite nod of her head toward the man, she proceeded up the four flights of stairs to the observation platform. Standing at the railing she could look westward to the ocean. The immensity of the trip that lay before her registered full force; making her feel very insignificant and vulnerable. Mentally shaking herself, she regained her composure. *One step at a time, Skipper. One step at a time.*

She let her eyes sweep to the mouth of Gray's Harbor where riprap jetties on both sides of the harbor's mouth formed a perfect opening for incoming boats. The bay opened up and became the shape of half an hourglass. As she turned east, she could make out Hoquiam and Aberdeen, which were mill and seafood towns. The bay, being about twenty miles in diameter, looked to be very shallow with the low tide exposing miles and miles of mud flats. Channels had been dredged and marked with buoys so deep-keeled ships coming from foreign ports could get to these two small cities to take on loads of logs, agriculture products, and sea food.

The fishing resort of Westport lay on the south side of the harbor's mouth: the fishing and vacation area of Ocean Shores to the north, and finally the immense shallow bay supported the crabbing industry. All this gave Gray's Harbor the badge of prosperity. The fishing resorts, once prosperous when salmon were plentiful, now featured the new tourist attraction, whale watching. Helen suddenly realized they hadn't seen a whale. She hoped that the whales hadn't become an endangered species like the salmon.

Intoxicated by all that lay before her, Helen reluctantly descended the four flights of stairs to pause and inspect the derelict seaman's wares. He sat quietly beside his pitifully small spread of shells depicting various ships. Helen determined to buy at least one shell, to make for certain he would eat today.

The dirty Greek fisherman's cap matched his dark, soiled clothing. His creased face had seen many storms and much wind and weather; the deep lines etched by wind and weather only partially obscured by a four-day growth of whiskers. A roll-your-own cigarette never left his mouth; he sucked in the smoke as a regular part of his shallow breathing.

Helen looked at each shell carefully, lending an air of importance to her final selection. She settled on a three-inch shell with an 18th century English Bark drawn on it having two masts and schooner rigged. On the shell was listed its type, name, and the year it was commissioned, also printed in India ink. "I'll take this one," Helen announced. "How much is it?"

The old vender looked at the shell and then at Helen. "That one is three dollars."

Hellen fished three dollar bills from her pocket. "Here you are; I like what you are doing. Is this what you do for a living?"

"Yes, I'm an artist," he said off-hand holding up a book. "I bought this book with pictures of ancient sailing ships. I use it as a guide."

"Have you always been an artist?"

"No, Ma'am, I used to be a sailor. I've sailed ships all over the world from 40 to 80 footers."

"What put you on the beach?"

"I just got too damn old for that life. This seemed to be as good a place as any to settle, so here I am." Offering his weather-wrinkled hand," he said, "I'm Arron Bradley."

"I'm Helen Davis, skipper of the Sea Witch." Helen extended her own hand.

"Really? A woman skipper; you don't see many of those. Where you headed?"

"Tahiti, by way of Peru."

"I'd sure like to be making that voyage again. You need a deck hand?"

Helen started to laugh but thought better of it. "No Bradley, I have a deck hand, in fact he's the owner. Up until now he's never been a sailor, but, he's learning fast, so we don't have room for another deck hand. We're a small ship, only thirty feet."

"Too bad. I'm getting tired of being on the beach. I think I could still carry my weight on a craft like yours. But, I like being an artist, though it's not much of a living."

"I'll be here a few days, Bradley. Perhaps we'll meet again, and I can look at more of your art."

"I'd like that, skipper. Maybe I'll see you on the docks. I'll keep an eye out for you."

Sauntering back to the marina, pausing now and then to peer into windows of tourist shops, Helen let her mind drift back to last night and Rodger. *After a leisurely steak dinner accompanied by a bottle of Cabernet Sauvignon wine, we returned to the Sea Witch. Rodger, preceding me down the steps, turned, and stood at the bottom waiting for me with outstretched arms.*

"Whoa, this is a surprise," I had said as I walked into those outstretched arms.

"I told you I wanted to be more than a friend," he reminded me. He then asked, "Do you want to be lovers?"

I had replied, "Yes, I do."

He kissed me passionately; I returned that kiss. He led me to the middle of the salon and kissed me passionately again. This time we met with their bodies as well as their lips. Rodger began to unbutton his shirt. I reached out and took his hand away from his shirtfront and said, "Let me do it. Don't you like to unwrap presents at Christmas time?"

He followed my lead by unbuttoning my blouse and softly whispered "Merry Christmas."

∗   ∗   ∗   ∗

CHAPTER 12

▼

The bus moved easily along the freeway as traffic was light for a Friday morning. Rodger sat by a window, enjoying the day, watching the rural scene unfold. The few passengers on the bus seemed lost in thought. Rodger let his own mind wander back to the previous night on the Sea Witch.

He had offered himself to Helen. She had accepted. Their relationship was on a new plane now. It had been a long time since Rodger had been intimate with Irene. There had never been anyone else since he and Irene had married. It had been awkward in the beginning with Helen. But their passion took over. They flowed into each other's world, each giving to the other until all they wanted to do was lie back and hold each other in the silence of the night. A gentle smile crossed Rodger's face as he relived those moments.

The rural scenery change to forested foothills, the road steepened considerably as they ascended the lower portion of the Olympic Mountain Range. On merging with I-5 in Olympia the traffic, though heavier, still moved steadily onward. After a short stop in downtown Olympia to change busses, Rodger was once more on his way. Arriving in Seatle on schedule, he spied Irene at the loading ramp beside the bus station. Making his way to her, he was surprised to be greeted by a familiar, if perfunctuary, hug and kiss.

"You look great, Rodger. I haven't seen you look this good in a long time. Life at sea must agree with you."

"Thanks for the compliment. You look good, too Irene. What is this court date about?" the two of them walked hurriedly to the parking lot.

Irene fumbled nervously with her purse, "As I told you on the phone, the judge wants to question us now before granting the legal separation, since you won't be available at the end of the usual 90 day waiting period."

"Well, I guess they're calling the shots. The two of us will see him tomorrow, right?"

"That's the plan." Irene slipped behind the stearing wheel of the car automatically.

"These past weeks have made a big change in my life, Irene, and I'm learning to be a sailor."

"So this Helen actually knows how to sail, I thought perhaps that was part of the big lie," replied Irene vindictively.

"Believe me, what I told you was true. Without her I'd be on the beach somewhere or worse. I didn't know how much skill was needed until we got underway. I don't think most people know how complicated sailing is." Rodger sat back and surveyed the city scene as they proceeded through the Seattle traffic to Bellevue.

Irene gripped the wheel, her eyes fixed on the road ahead. "Are you sleeping with her?"

"If you had asked me that two days ago, the answer would have been, no," Rodger replied reluctantly. "However, the situation has changed. I'm sure you didn't want to hear that, but you asked, and I want to be truthful with you. If we hadn't filed for legal separation, the answer would have been different."

"I've been having second thoughts about the legal separation," Irene spoke with determination in her voice. "This may complicate things for you and your lover, but I've decided I don't want a legal separation."

"What made you change your mind?" Rodger asked with agitation in his voice.

"I think this is a fling with you and Helen. I think your fear of tuberculosis is affecting your power of reasoning," Helen spoke angrily. "I'm your wife who has given you thirty years of my life, three sons, and helped you build a successful business. I don't think this Helen-come-lately deserves any of the rewards."

"What about this court date?" Rodger looked directly at Irene as she looked straight ahead.

"We won't need to keep it, unless you plan to fight me or want a divorce."

Rodger stared out the car windshield. "No," he said picking his words carefully. "I won't fight you, at least not now. I have a voyage to complete. If I succeed, I'll be asking for a divorce. If I don't succeed, there's no need for either a legal separation or divorce…is there. However, if I don't make it, for what-ever reason, I want Helen to have the Sea Witch. Is that understood?"

"Agreed." Said Irene with a sigh of relief. "I'll call our lawyer when we get home and have him cancel the court date."

"When did you come to this decision?" Rodger turned again to study Irene's face.

"Oh, I've been thinking about it for several days, but I made up my mind about five minutes ago. I'm angry and disappointed, but I'm more convinced then ever legal separation is not the answer. At the end of the voyage will be time enough to settle our relationship."

"I can live with that, Irene. I understand your anger, but I have anger too. I think we've disappointed each other. It's never just one person, is it?"

* * * *

After sleeping the night again in the guest bedroom, Rodger awakened early next morning to the sounds of the neighborhood coming to life: children's voices at play, a car starting its engine and backing out a long driveway, and the sound of someone moving about in the kitchen. After showering and dressing, he walked a familiar path to the kitchen. "Good morning, Irene. That coffee smells wonderful; you Swedes do know how to make a good cup of coffee."

Irene ~~Helen~~ was startled as she sat at the kitchen table reading the morning paper, "Thanks, it helps start the day. When do you plan to go back, Rodger?

"Tomorrow, today we can concentrate on the business. We need to get Junior in the driver's seat." Pouring himself a cup of coffee, Rodger straddled the chair he'd pulled away from the kitchen table. "I'm not trying to justify my actions, Irene. But I would like you to know my reasoning, understand where I'm coming from. When Dr. Smith gave me a year or less to live, I came to believe that desperate times required desperate action. That's when the trip to Tahiti, my lifetime dream, resurfaced. Unfortunately, it resurfaced in an older man's body, but it gave me the distraction I needed. I knew you and the family would try to talk me out of it, that's why I prepared for the voyage in secret. It became my obsession, helped me deal with the illness. Helen, or anyone like her, was not a part of the original plan. But she is an important part of it now."

"You certainly are living out your fantasy. If that's made these last months better for you, I'll try to understand, though I don't like it. Maybe we can both live out our fantasies in our remaining time."

"How are you coming with your painting?"

"It's on hold until Junior takes over the business. As you say, we need to get Junior in the driver's seat."

"When do you want to turn it over to him?"

"Immediately. Why don't we go to the office after breakfast and take care of our unfinished business with Junior. You can say goodbye to our employees. I'm sure they'd love to see you, again."

"Good idea. Let's eat, then make your phone call, and I'll get ready to go to the office."

Irene called their lawyer and brought him up to date. He thought it a good idea they postpone the legal separation. He agreed to call the judge and cancel the hearing.

* * * *

Downtown Bellevue was busy as usual. As Rodger pulled into his old reserve parking spot, he discovered he had mixed feelings about returning to the office. It was a natural, comfortable thing to do, but he was happy it was only a visit. He wouldn't trade his old life at the mortgage company for his new life on the Sea Witch.

On seeing Rodger enter with Irene, Sylvia, the receptionist, exploded with a happy shriek that drew the attention of all the employees. All four office workers converged on Rodger mimicking Sylvia's reception. It was a festive reunion for all. Rodger had always been not only a good employer, but a friend as well.

A phone call to a local bakery brought a box of pastries, someone put on the coffee pot. The next half hour was filled with questions and answers about his trip. Rodger was careful to avoid any mention of the skipper of the Sea Witch or that she was a woman.

Rodger, Irene, and Junior excused themselves and sought the privacy of Irene's office. The employees took this as a signal to return to work. Irene did not sit at her desk, but invited Junior to take her chair. Now that they were in private, Junior's first question was, "I thought you had a court date. What happened?"

Irene replied, "We canceled it. It wasn't necessary since we've decided to drop the legal separation proceedings."

Before Junior could register surprise or question them further, "We have a surprise for you." Rodger replied before Irene could continued.

"I haven't liked your surprises lately," replied Junior cautiously.

"Your mother and I want to retire, but we don't want to sell the business. We want to keep the business and have you manage it for us."

"I am surprised. I guess I expected to manage this for you two in your old age, but not this soon. Of course I'll manage it, but why do you want to retire, Mother? You're not old or ill, like Dad."

"Hey," replied Rodger. "I'm ill, not old. But then, I guess health is a better measurement of age then chronological years."

"Sorry Dad, a slip of the tongue." Junior showed discomfort at his remark.

"I'm delighted that you're willing to manage the company and probably, someday, own it," said Rodger. "This business has been our baby, we've nurtured it for twenty-seven years. It's prosperous, and we want to keep it in the family."

Irene joined in, "I'm pleased too, dear. You'll have to hire another employee to take your place, as you will be replacing me. I suppose you could ask your brothers, but they both have other chosen fields, not this business. I doubt they'd want to re-direct their careers, but you're the manager; do as you like."

"I don't think either would be interested, Junior agreed, but I'll ask. If you will it to the three of us, and it needs to be sold to cash them out, I would want the first-right-of-refusal when it goes up for sale. That way it would stay in the family."

Rodger looked relieved, "That's settled then; we'll have our lawyer do the paper work, and wrap this up."

"Great!" said Junior excitedly.

"I agree," replied Irene. She walked over and put her arm around Junior as Rodger stayed seated but smiling approval.

※ ※ ※ ※

The next morning Rodger said his goodbyes, and Junior drove him to the bus station. They arrived just as the long, gray Trailways transporter rounded the corner. Parking the car, the two men walked in silence to the loading zone where Rodger turned and embraced his son. "You're the head of the family while I'm gone, son," his voice husky with emotion,. "Look after your mother. She's not always as strong as she sounds." The bus for Olympia pulled up and Rodger stepped aboard as he gave a goodbye wave to Junior.

The miles sped by transporting Rodger back into his newfound role of sailor and companion; a man who was fulfilling a fantasy with the help of his new soul mate.

   *   *   *   *

CHAPTER 13
▼

Deciding to indulge in the luxury of sleeping in while Rodger was gone, Helen snuggled down into the warm, double sleeping bag. She stretched her graceful, athletic body, like a house cat might, enjoying the warmth and coziness of their bed. The slap-slap of the waves on the hull eventually lured her back to sleep. Re-awakening at nine o'clock she continued to lie there, smiling to herself as she once again reviewed the quick turn of events in their relationship. *Rodger is a passionate lover who has taken me to the mountaintop. Who could ask for more?*

Rolling out of bed, she stretched again. Glancing at herself in the mirror, she smiled, *who would have thought after this long year without Clyde, I would find myself in love with another man...a man who's dying.* That last thought quickly shattered Helen's happy mood. Dressing in clean dungarees, polo shirt, and sneakers, she threw a sweatshirt around her shoulders; the idea of breakfast ashore gave her spirits a lift.

Cowboy Bob's looks like a place where I could get a hearty breakfast, Helen decided, and chose a seat at the counter grabbing a menu as she passed the cash register. The waitress carrying a coffee pot, paused in front of her and looked at her inquisitively, "This what you want?" Helen nodded. After studying the menu for a minute, she settled for sausage and eggs. The coffee went down easily, having a robustness that put an arch in her back. There's n*othing like a good cup of coffee to start the day off right.*

After breakfast Helen continued her walk up Main Street, amused as she read the hype that appeared in nearly every store window. It was all about whales and whale watching. At the end of the street she found herself drawn once again to the four-story observation tower. Sure enough, there was Bradley Arron sitting, eyes closed, with his wares spread out on one of the four tower cement pedestals. It was apparent he faced the sun to inhale the heat of it into his timeworn body.

Helen greeted him with a cheery, "Hello."

Bradley opened his eyes, his face wrinkling into a characature of a smile. "Hello, yourself. I knew you'd be back."

"How did you know?" Helen stood looking at his shells on display picking them up and turning them over to study the backs as well as the front of the shell.

He peered intently into her eyes, then, in a croaking voice: "We sailors have a way of knowing things, especially when it comes to women."

"Why, Bradley, you sound like a ladies man," Helen's voice became warm with pleasure.

He grinned, still with the homemade cigarette in his lips: "I had my day in the sun. Had a girl in every port mosta my life; never married one though. How're you doing with your boat repairs?"

"Nothing is happening yet, the parts won't be here until tomorrow. John Day is coming aboard about noon today for a look-see. He's doing the installation of our radar, navigation system and auto pilot."

"John's a real pro." Bradley slowly and with apparent pain stood facing Helen.

"One never knows about the quality of work you're going to get when traveling. By the way, you said you had other art works to show me. Did you bring them?"

"No, but you can come to my place to see them, if you'd like," suggested Aaron smiling.

"If you think I'd go home with a sailor who had a girl in every port, you're sadly mistaken."

Bradley's face shone with pleasure at the trend of the conversation. "Well, this old salt has been in dry dock for a long time, you'd be safe with me. But by the looks of you, kid, I think you can take care of yourself."

"I'll take that as a compliment, Aaron. Call me Helen."

"It was meant to be a compliment, Helen. How do you like the new shells I have today?"

"I like this one especially; the picture on it is similar to the Sea Witch."

"Well then, it's yours." Aaron straightened to his full height, thrusting his shoulders back in pride.

"Oh, no. I couldn't do that. How much is it?" Helen was taken back by this turn of events.

"I want to give it to you. I'm not so damn poor I can't give a friend a gift."

"Well, okay. I'll take it as a token of our friendship. I really do like it."

Helen took the shell and carefully put it in her shopping bag. "I've got to go now and get ready for John Day. I may see you tomorrow." Helen turned to leave. "Thanks for the gift."

"Goodbye Helen. Tomorrow I'll bring some of my particularly well-done shells."

She gave him a lighthearted hand salute, "See you later sailor." Strolling back through crowds of tourists taking in the carnival atmosphere of Westport, Helen let the sights and smells flood her senses.

✳ ✳ ✳ ✳

John Day arrived shortly before noon, and Helen invited him aboard to size up the job. "Do you want the radar installed, in the cockpit or below deck?" John sat down on the bench seat as he sized up the configuration of the cockpit.

"In the cockpit." Helen said after a moment's hesitation.

"How about the navigation system?" John looked up at Helen as she stood at the back of the cockpit.

"Let's put it in the cockpit too." Helen had determined she wanted everything as handy as possible.

"I see you have an externally mounted tiller; it should be easy to install the auto-steering. I'll pick the parts up at Westport Marine tomorrow, and be here about ten o'clock if the freight truck's on time." John rose in order to speak directly at Helen.

"Sounds good." Helen extended her hand and smiled a goodbye.

After he left, Helen took stock of their situation. *If Rodg gets his court date on Monday, he should be here on Tuesday, and we can be on our way. That's assuming John is able to successfully install the new add-on's without any problems and Rodger resolves his court problem. In the meantime I'll think positive and fill the larder so we'll be ready to sail.*

*　　*　　*　　*

Chapter 14

Rodger's bus ride back to Westport was uneventful. He was eager to see Helen and his new home, the Sea Witch. Striding the length of the dock to the slip where he'd left the Sea Witch in its double slip beside the "Lone Star", he stopped dead in his tracks. *The Sea Witch isn't here! Have I mistaken the moorage? No, this is the right slip. There's the Lone Star, but an empty space beside it. Perhaps the harbormaster moved us to another slip. Easy Rodg…keep control of yourself; there's probably no problem."*

Rodger looked for a place to stash his overnight satchel. Knowing the owner of the Lone Star wouldn't mind, he tossed his satchel on board. As he turned to leave, a spasm of deep, chest coughing convulsed him. Clinging to the gunnels until the coughing subsided, he was still unsteady when he hurried to the marina office building. Surveying the marina standing looking out the window, it was a moment before the harbormaster became aware someone had entered the office. "What can I do for you?"

"I'm Rodger McCauley. Have you moved my boat from slip A-20 to another location?" Rodger stood at the office counter trying not to appear upset.

"No, why do you ask?"

"My boat's gone and it shouldn't be," Rodger blurted. "I have a partner, but I don't think she would take it out without me." Rodger showed nervousness now as he tried to unravel the mystery.

"Is that the boat John Day is working on?"

"It could be, my partner was to have navigation, self-steering, and radar systems installed. Does John Day do that type of work?" Rodger asked.

"Yes. Maybe he and your partner took it out for a shake-down cruise."

"That's possible…I'm upset because when I returned from a trip to Seattle, I found our slip vacant. I guess all I can do is wait for awhile to see if that's what's going on."

Rodger walked the length of the marina back to the slip, wanting to believe this was the solution to the mystery. He thought of other possibilities, but nothing else made sense. The smell of frying bacon from a nearby boat reminded him he hadn't eaten since breakfast. He stopped at the first restraunt he came to, Cowboy Bob's.

The waitress took his order and poured him a cup of coffee. "You look like you've lost your best friend," she ventured reading his face.

"Well, I'm not sure I haven't, but I didn't realize it showed. I came back from Seattle today expecting my boat and my partner to be waiting for me. Both are gone and I'm worried. The harbormaster thinks my partner and a local mechanic may have taken it for a shakedown cruise."

"What's the name of you boat?" the waitress asked as she made a mental connection.

"Sea Witch. Why?" Rodger sat at the counter looking across at the waitress.

"Well, I think I've met your partner, if it's a woman."

"My partner and Skipper is a woman."

"She's been in for breakfast the past three days. Her name is Helen, right?"

Rodger brightened, "You know Helen? Did she say anything about going out in the boat today?"

"No, but I think I saw your boat, a Tahiti Ketch, go out about noon. I can see the Marina entrance from here and a ketch rounded the farther-most marker buoy heading north."

"Was she alone or with someone?" Rodger showed some signs of relief.

"I only saw one person, but it didn't look like Helen." The waitress stepped to the kitchen to place Rodger's order. She returned with the food to find Rodger deep in thought. "Here, this should make you feel better. Do you want ketchup for those fries?"

"Yes, please. I guess all I can do is wait." Rodger's mind raced. *Why wasn't Helen on deck if it was the Sea Witch? Or at the tiller? Is something wrong? Am I letting my imagination run away with me? Could this John Day have been at the tiller, trying out the new auto-navigation system? Could Helen have stepped below deck?* Frantic thoughts flooded his mind.

Rodger ate his hamburger and drank his coffee in silence. When he finished he thanked the waitress for the information and walked quickly across the street to a vantage point where he could see if the Sea Witch had returned. His spirits sank when, once again, he looked at the empty slip. He thought, *I could climb to the top of the observation tower by the breakwater, maybe I can spot them if they're in the harbor.*

Upon approaching the tower, Rodger noticed an old shell peddler located at one of the pedestals of the tower with his wares spread out. Climbing the stairs, he reached the observation platform only to have his body racked with coughing and convulsing forcing him to his knees. After a few minutes when he was finally able to stand, he surveyed the expanse of the harbor. Being summer, there were a lot of boats out. Eight were sailboats, two of them were ketch-rigged, but too far away to determine if one was the Sea Witch. Turning ninety degrees, his eyes swept over the ocean view. A few larger commercial fishing boats were plying the coastline north and south. None resembled the Sea Witch.

He rested for a few moments, allowing his breathing to return to normal. Scanning the waters to the north, he spotted a small boat near the middle of Gray's Harbor. *There's one that looks like the Sea Witch!* He took the steps down from the top of the observation tower with a surge of new energy and lifted spirits.

Buoyed up with new hope and anticipation, he hurried back to the marina. He contemplated going back to the slip to wait, but decided against it. There's no view of the harbor from the slip. The ketch was definitely headed for the marina as it tacked starboard, then to port, making her way into the wind.

His fears quieted allowing himself to became aware of the beauty of the day. Letting his body soak in the welcome warmth of the sun, he noticed the counter-cooling effect of the wind. Chiding himself for being upset when confronted with the possibility of losing Helen and his dream, he realized this had become his real purpose for living.

Beside him a tourist scanned the ocean panarama through a pair of binoculars. "Quite a view," the man remarked.

"Yes it is magnificent," Rodger replied and realized the solution to his problem was close at hand. "Would you mind letting me use your binoculars for a moment? I'm looking for my boat that's out on a sea-trial; I'm concerned about her arrival."

Hesitating, the tourist extended the glasses toward Rodger. "You'll probably have to adjust them, as I am near sighted."

Rodger carefully put the binoculars to his eyes, making a slight correction. The view that came into focus made his heart leap for joy. "It's my Sea Witch," he shouted. "There she is!" Rodger instantly felt the tension drain from his body, and gratefully handed the binoculars back to the tourist. "This calls for a celebration. Can I buy you a beer or something while I wait for my boat to make port?"

"No thanks. I'm with my family, they should be along any minute."

Rodger all but ran the distance back to slip A-20, savoring the moment when he and Helen would embrace. *I haven't felt this way since I was a young man; perhaps some things don't change after all.*

He made his way down the gangplank to the floating dock with the empty slip. Retrieving his satchel from the deck of the Lone Star, he used it for a pillow as he stretched out on the dock to await the return of the Sea Witch. The sun felt so good he hadn't known how tired he was brought about by the bus ride and his apprehension. *Perhaps a little nap is what I need now.*

Rodger became aware of a face just inches from his. Opening his eyes he saw Helen kneeling over him laughing, and about to kiss him awake. *Okay, have it your way,* he thought closing his eyes so she could do just that. When he felt her lips touch his lips he reached out with his arms quickly encircling her back, "Welcome home," he whispered.

John Day stood watching the scene with amusement. "Everything checks out and she's ready to go whenever you are."

"Great! How much do I owe you?" Rodger rose to his feet, his arm around Helen's waist.

"Five hours labor at fifty dollars an hour adds up to two hundred seventy one dollars with tax. Also, I will accept a check, Westport Marine vouched for your credit."

"I appreciate that." Rodger wrote the check and handed it to John Day. "Thanks for giving us such good service."

"You're welcome; happy sailing to Tahiti."

"Thanks again. This new equipment will help make it possible." As John walked back down the dock, Rodger turned to Helen, "Are you ready to leave with the morning tide?"

"You bet. Evidently the court date worked out alright. Helen paused when Rodger didn't respond. I'll take you to dinner tonight," she offered. "You can tell me all about it. The Sea Witch is ready to leave, I've filled the larder for a week's sailing. That should get us as far as central California."

"Sounds good to me, but let's go below now and I'll bring you up-to-date on my trip to Bellevue, plus we have other things to talk about."

Taking Rodger's hand, Helen led him aboard the Sea Witch saying, "That's kind of what I had in mind. The other things to talk about."

* * * *

CHAPTER 15

▼

It was early when Rodger awoke. The sun would'nt make its appearance above the horizon for another thirty minutes. He glanced at Helen, her back to him now, still wrapped in sleep. Reluctant to awaken her, Rodger focused his attention on the cabin's interior. *The lovely, warm patina of the rich mahogany comes only with care and age*, he decided. His gaze shifted to the kerosene lantern suspended above the table, swaying slightly as the boat rocks. *Gimbeled, isn't that what Helen called it? Gimbeled, both the lantern and the cook stove, allowing them to swing with the roll of the Sea Witch.*

The morning sun, brightly illuminating the far wall of the cabin, awakened Helen. She could feel Rodger's warm body beside her, but she remained still allowing herself to enter slowly into the day. Memories, still lingering from the night before, reminded her of their conversation over dinner. Irene's refusal to agree to a legal separation until the journey to Tahiti was completed. *Dear, sweet Rodger* thought Helen, *he'd been so worried about her reaction; how it would affect their relationship. If the truth were to be known, she, didn't know how she felt about it. A legal separation hadn't been an issue when she set out on this trip with Rodger; hadn't been a factor when she fell in love with him. That was really all that mattered now anyway. She was in love with him.* Rolling over, she snuggled within Rodger's outstretched arm.

Rodger's arm quickly encircled Helen, drawing her body close to his. Silently they both savored the moment. Then reaching down with his free hand, Rodger gently turned Helen's face toward his, gazed tenderly into her eyes and whispered softly, "Where's my morning Coffee?"

"What a romantic you are, Mr. McCauley. I'll make a deal with you. I'll put on the coffee, if you'll make the breakfast."

"You're the captain." Helen rolled out of bed while Rodger indulged himself in the pleasure of watching her lithe, nude body gilded by the morning sun; move gracefully aft to the bathroom. Pulling on his shorts he said, "You go to the showers while I do coffee and breakfast; I'll shower later. We won't get a shower for a couple of days while we're at sea, so make the most of it. Incidently, where is our next port-of-call?"

"Newport, Oregon, it's 150 nautical miles south; usually a two-day run depending on the wind. This will be our shake-down cruise for the new equipment."

Upon returning to the salon area, Helen planted a kiss on the back of his neck as he stood facing the galley. She slipped into yesterday's clothes, "I'm off to the showers" she called out from the top of the stairs carrying her toiletries and fresh clothing.

After Helen's return they ate a leisurely breakfast, even tarried over a second cup of coffee. But the tide change was in two hours, so Rodger had no choice but to bundle up his toiletries and clothing and head for the showers. While the water heated for the dishes, Helen made a quick check of the rigging, sails, and electronics. Returning to the cabin, she converted the bed back into a divan and once again the salon was their chart room, dining room, kitchen, and living room.

Since Rodger had joined her in the salon for sleeping, the v-berth near the bow made a good place to store bulk food, foul weather gear, extra sails, and storage for their sleeping bags now permanently zipped together.

Rodger returned from his shower and immediately joined in the preparation for departure. "According to the Canadian weather report, we're going to have a good sailing day for our journey south. The wind is out of the northwest from 5 to 15 knots, with morning clouds and a possible weather front from the south later in the afternoon."

"That sounds like a go; start the engine Rodg. I'll stow the loose things and meet you on deck." Quickly clearing the stove and table, she joined Rodger. Taking the jib out of the sail bag, Rodger readied it to hoist, then removed the ties around the flaked main and mizzen sail. The engine idled smoothly, Helen took command of the tiller and signaled Rodger to cast off the three mooring lines and bring in the bumpers. Pushing the throttle into reverse gear, they slowly backed out of the slip into the main waterway leading out of the marina.

Once they cleared the marina entrance, Helen signaled Rodger to hoist the mainsail, jib, and mizzen sail. Helen allowed the boat to fall off the wind until the sails filled. Rodger then cut the engine and the Sea Witch, with the wind coming over her starboard side, was sailing on a broad reach. Rodger felt a warm surge of pride at how well he now performed his nautical duties. Glancing toward Helen, he saw her smile and nod approval. He grinned back, all was well in the world.

"I can see the breaker line dead ahead of us," shouted Rodger. "It's slack tide."

"Good. Restart the engine in case we need it. Then come back here and join me in the cockpit. We'll stay on a broad reach until we get clear of the harbor opening for about a quarter-mile, then we'll make our turn south." The wind held steady as the hull glided through the frothing bar line without a hitch. Relaxing at the tiller, Helen looked happy.

"That was nice sailing, Skipper. What do you want me to do now?"

"We're out far enough for our turn, so cut the engine and be ready to trim the main, mizzen, and jib sheets. According to our new navigation system we need to be running as close to 210 degrees as possible."

Rodger trimmed the sheets on the three sails, the Sea Witch picked up the wind's rhythm. Scanning the water, Rodger could see the two-foot waves were quickly becoming three-foot waves. The Sea Witch was handling the waves well so he went below to heat the leftover coffee from breakfast.

While the coffee was heating, Rodger sat down and turned the marine radio to the weather station. The voice coming from the radio sounded American not Canadian; that meant they had sailed into the range of the station in Oregon. The announcer proclaimed small craft warnings for coastal area, with a front moving in from the southwest. According to the forcast, there would be waves to four feet with wind from 25 to 35 miles per hour.

Rodger filled two mugs and returned to the cockpit to find Helen intent upon a new development. The Sea Witch broke through the waves now with spray coming over the rails.

Calling out over the sound of the rising wind, Helen shouted, "Set the mugs in the holder by the hatch and bring up the foul weather gear and storm jib. This is going to get sloppy."

Rodger stowed the cups and made a quick dash for the v-berth below deck where the gear was stored. Arms bulging with their yellow slickers, boots, hats, and life jackets, Rodger made his way back up the steps to the cockpit. Taking over the tiller, Helen pulled on her bib overalls, slipped into her jacket and ten-inch high rubber boots. After adding sou'wester hat, and life jacket to her ensemble, she took the helm while Rodger struggled into his own gear.

Braced at the tiller, Helen faced into the sharpening wind. "Douse the jib and mizzen, and bend on the storm jib," she shouted above the rigging noise. "That'll give us steerage. Then lower the mainsail some and we'll start tying reefing knots to reduce its size. Flake the mizzen and lash it securely to its boom. Stow the jib sail in the sail bag, and put it below so it's off the foredeck. Then secure the forward hatch."

"Aye, Aye Captain," replied Rodger with a look of admiration on his face. He went quickly about his assigned work and in twenty minutes had the Sea Witch prepared for rough weather. After Helen's nod of approval, they sat with the tiller between them prepared to face the oncoming squall.

Salt spray peppered their faces as it came over the rails and bow. Sheets of rain drenched them, but they were dry inside their rain gear. The cockpit, although self-bailing, soon filled ankle deep with water. The squall enveloped them. Wind ripping at their rubberized jackets, water splashing at their feet, running in torrents from their sou'westers down their back. Helen clung tightly to the tiller fighting to keep the Sea Witch on course, with defiance and laughter in her eyes…and then, it was over. The wind died down like someone had turned off a giant fan, the rain became a drizzle, then stopped altogether. Helen and Rodger stared at one another for a moment. Grinning, Rodger reached over and wiped away a drop of water dripping from Helen's nose. Her eyes...so intense a moment before, crinkled at the corners. They burst into laughter.

Rodger stood to better survey the ocean about them. "What happened to our sunny day?"

"That's the way the weather is on the ocean, Rodg. These squalls and fronts come up out of nowhere, giving a thrilling ride, a good soaking, pass on through, then 'voila' everything is fine again."

Rodger added, "Wasn't it Barkley that seventeenth century philosopher, who said, 'the sublime is experienced through terror; not through pleasant happenings and surroundings.' For a brief moment I felt the sublime, I think you did too."

"You've got that right. If you'll take the helm, I'll go below, get out of my gear, and put on some fresh coffee."

At the helm Rodger, sat back and marveled at how the squall disappear as quickly as it came. The self-bailing cockpit had only an inch of water in it now. Then without warning a spasm of coughing tore through his lungs, robbed him of breath and doubled him over. He gripped the tiller until his coughing subsided. Then lay back exhausted, thankful that Helen wasn't there to be a witness to this. It was difficult to believe that just a few minutes ago he'd been racing around the deck handling an emergency, and now the weather was relatively calm.

Helen, returning to the cockpit with hot coffee, sat down next to Rodger. He tried to hide his exhaustion brought on by the coughing spasm. However, Helen saw the strain in his face and his lack of strength in the hand on the tiller. "You've had one of your spells, haven't you?"

"Yes, but I'm O.K. now."

"Are they getting any better?"

"They don't happen as often, but they seem as intense. It's such a nuisance. If I get worse, I'll let you know. I'm taking my medication faithfully, so all I need beyond that is fresh air, sunshine, and you."

"Maybe having me is part of your problem. We've been pretty intense."

"Our relationship is more important to me than anything; I'm just fine…most of the time. Let's forget my health and enjoy the trip. Okay?"

"I can do that, but I want you to be up front with me, Rodg. We're in this together and I want to know what's going on at all times. Have I made myself clear?"

"Crystal, Skipper. I'll tell you if I have a turn for the worse…or for the better. I hate laying this health burden on you."

"I came into this with my eyes open, so put your guilt away, it has no place here."

"Aye, aye Skipper. By the way, does a sailor ever get to call his Captain 'Sweetheart'?"

"Only after lights out."

✳ ✳ ✳ ✳

The waves receded now to a one-foot chop, the wind lessened to 10 knots, the Sea Witch had regained her former rhythm. Rodger replaced the storm jib with the Genoa jib, took the reefing knots out of the mainsail, and re-hoisted it to the top of the mast. He then added the mizzen sail.

The sky cleared as the sun reached its zenith; its warmth caused steam to rise from the wet deck and cabin roof. Occasionally a fish jumped and squawking sea birds swooped low looking for a handout; when none was offered, went on their way looking elsewhere for the next meal. Now and then a harbor seal poked its shiny black head out of the waves to stare wide-eyed at the passing boat. Life forms appeared everywhere about them, everything seemed right with the world.

It was time for lunch again; Rodger emerged from below with a tray containing two generous sandwiches, chips, and beer. "I hope you like my specialty sandwich."

"I'm sure I will Mate. What is it? All I see is lettuce from here."

"I call it Rodger McCauley special, it's one of my favorites and easy to fix. It's peanut butter, mayonnaise, and lettuce."

"Well the proof is in the tasting; hand me a half and I'll let my taste buds be the judge. Mmm, Good. You do have a way with food, Rodg."

After lunch Helen looked over at Rodger who was stretch out on the benchseat. "Do you feel rested enough to take over the tiller? I need to go below for a nap, it's going to be a long night. I won't be sleeping while our new steering device handles the boat at night."

"I'm fine, really, Rodger insisted. Sweet dreams, Skipper." Helen hesitated, and then disappeared into the cabin. Sitting beside the tiller, Rodger's mind drifting back over the past few weeks. *I've learned a lot about sailing from Helen. But more important, I'm in love with her. In this short time we've changed from being strangers to lovers. I've returned home twice and I think Irene and I have finally come to an understanding regarding our relationship. She no longer considers me a runaway, nor does the family feel that way. I'm gad I returned home and straightened that out.*

My health is still an unknown factor; I look healthier and feel stronger in most ways, but the tuberculosis hadn't gone away. Am I better? I wished I'd taken time to see Dr. Smith when I was in Bellevue. The trip to Tahiti, so far, has exceeded my wildest expectations. I never thought there would be another woman in my life. And what a woman she is. She has strength I can draw on, if need be. I know I'm not a coward, but I've never dealt with death looking over my shoulder before.

Rodger had always loved the sea, and this journey intensified that feeling. He now realized Helen, too, was on a quest. She yearned for an escape from loneliness and boredom. He seriously doubted Helen had been looking for another man in her life after her beloved Clyde died. He'd certainly never expected there'd be another woman in his life. Yet here they were, two middle-aged people, head-over-heels in love, and acting and feeling like they were twenty-year-olds. Rodger tried to project his thinking ahead, to the end of the journey. But his mind refused. He had today.

*   *   *   *

Chapter 16

Helen lay awake on the divan; the sleep she sought eluded her. The magnitude of her responsibility on this voyage, their safety, was a challenge she had never experienced before. Their lives were at stake, and even though she rationalized they were expendable, her survival instinct and her desire to succeed remained paramount. In addition, she and Rodger, now a twosome, held hope of having some time together. She was thankful she had admitted to Rodger her need for help: with navigation, thus the G.P.S.; for help at the tiller, thus the autopilot system; and a ship-to shore radio as a means of communicating with the outside world. These additions would help keep them from ending up a statistic in the coast guard category, "lost at sea." Rodger never hesitated when he put up the money needed for the job.

In all kinds of weather the GPS system would give accurate worldwide fixes 24 hours a day, and having it interface with the autopilot practically added a crew member aboard who took over the helm much of the time. This phantom crewmember possessed a genius mind for navigation by receiving signals sent by high altitude satellite, determining their location within 6 meters, 95% of the time. Helen felt their chances to succeed on the Sea Witch were now greatly improved. *Rodger has such faith in me. I hope I'm worthy of his trust* she fretted before sleep finally eased her burden.

* * * *

"Helen, can you come up here?"

She woke with a start. "What's wrong?"

"You'll want to see this. Nothing is wrong, but this is something unusual. I think I'm looking at the topside of a whale."

Helen bolted up the stairway. Fifty yards off to starboard lay a mottled, gray hulk apparently with no beginning, no end.

"It just emerged out of the ocean and now it's sinking back into the ocean. There is a gaping hole on the top of the hulk spouting a spray of water into the air."

"Yep, that's what it is, a great gray whale, just basking in the sun. The blow hole enables it to stay like that for long periods of time." Helen held on to a shroud while she balanced on the gunnels for her observation point.

"It must be eighty feet long. I can't see its head or tail; nor do I want to." Rodger stood close to Helen while the new instruments ran the ship.

"Good thinking, Rodg. Let it sleep. It's luckier than some people I know."

"Oh…Okay, I get your point…go back to sleep. I promise I will awaken you only if we have a major emergency."

Helen went below and lay back on the divan. *How like a little boy he is in some ways; of course that could be said about most men. Rodg is such a dear, but he can be strong when the situation requires it.* She drifted back to sleep.

Rodger watched the weathervane device attached to the tiller react to the navigation display on the GPS dial. *Makes me feel like a passenger on the Sea Witch rather than being in command,* he mused. *The instruction booklet on the GPS did list a few things that it couldn't do, like yell, "Man overboard." Well, I guess we just must avoid falling overboard.*

That got Rodger to thinking about what he would do if Helen fell overboard, or vice versa. *I would keep an eye on her, jibe the boat, and come back on a beat. Then I would have to fish her out, but how? If she were wearing a life jacket it would be easier, Helen would remain buoyant. If the water was kicking up, and it probably would be because she wouldn't go over the side in calm water, I would need a pole with a hook on the end to get her to the side of the boat. With her help, I could get her aboard, but what if she were injured or knocked out by being hit by a jibing boom? How would I get her back aboard? I'll have to run this by Helen when she awakens. Come to think of it, she would have a harder time getting me back aboard than I would have with her. I must outweigh her by forty pounds.*

I've seen other sailboats at the marina, and they have a lifeline type of railing around the gunnels of the boat and the crewmembers wear a harness with a line attached to it and tied to a bolt secured to the main structure of the boat. Maybe when we reach Newport, Oregon we'll need to do a little more fitting out for this trans-ocean trip. Right now we only had life jackets and a coast guard approved emergency kit. What if we have to abandon ship? Would the dingy be sufficient for the open ocean?

Helen's appearance at the cabin opening interrupted Rodger's pondering. "Well, whale watcher, I had a good nap; I should be able to take the first and third watch tonight."

"Tell me about that?" Rodger slid over on the bench seat in the cockpit making room for Helen to sit.

"We'll both be up until dark. I'll take the tiller, or I should say I'll sit by the tiller and watch it steer itself with the aid of the autopilot and the GPS navigation system from eight o'clock until twelve o'clock. Then I'll awaken you, so you'll do the same from twelve o'clock until four o'clock. You then awaken me, and I'll take the third watch from four o'clock until eight o'clock. By then you'll be awake and have fixed breakfast, she smiled impishly. Then it's all yours until I finish the rest of my night's sleep."

"Sounds like a plan, Skipper. I'll go below and fix dinner to fortify us for our first night at sea."

Rodger retreated to the galley and opened the icebox hoping to get an inspiration for dinner. A pound of hamburger sat on the top shelf. *It's been awhile since we've had gourmet hamburger patties.* Grabbing the makings for a salad, he closed the lid on the icebox, noting the need to take on more ice at the next port-of-call, Newport, Oregon. Once they were making their crossing to Tahiti there probably wouldn't be opportunity for the gourmet meals he'd been serving. He planned to wine and dine Helen for as long as he could.

Spreading the dinner ingredients on the small counter, he hummed to himself as he put the dinner together. Starting with a salad of lettuce, tomatoes, and green chopped onions and bellpepper, he added a salad dressing of crumbled blue cheese, soybean oil, apple cider vinegar, sugar, and salt spices.

The salad called for white wine, like a Chardonnay, the beef for a Pinot Noir. They had both. With the table set and dinner nearly ready, Rodger called out through the hatch and in his best head waiter's voice announced, "Dinner is served, my Captain."

"Give me five minutes to make sure everything is shipshape, topside." Helen checked the trim of the three sails, the GPS screen, and the autopilot. The weather was stable, the wind steady out of the northwest at ten knots, and the temperature moderate. Satisfied everything was as it should be, Helen descended the steps into the salon. Rodger stood at the bottom step with open arms, Helen walked easily into his embrace. After a long, tender kiss she turned her attentiuon to dinner. "Let the festivities begin. With a spread like this we'll have to take it to the cockpit so we can linger over it and watch the helm at the same time."

"Okay, Killjoy." Rodger put the salad, bread and wine on a tray and carried it topside. Helen followed carrying the wine bottle.

"It all looks so inviting," she called out over her shoulder as she ascended the steps topside. The evening air was cool, but not cold. The sun was near the horizon and the seabirds were on their way home for the night, it was an ideal setting for their floating restraunt.

Rodger placed the tray between them on the bench seat. "This meal is a meal to celebrate the third member of this crew. We'll have to give it a name."

"You're talking about the autopilot and the GPS combination? That will take some thought. In the meantime this salad looks inviting, I'm eating."

"This is a salad dressing I tried to copy from a French cheese store. Ironically, we are near the Oregon coast where it was originated, Tillamook, Oregon. We're just off the Columbia River right now, so we'll pass Tillamook during the night."

"After tasting this dressing, Rodg, I'd say you did a good job, and the wine is a perfect match for the bleu cheese taste." Rodger smiled in appreciation. "What can you tell me about this part of the world?" Helen continued. "Geography was never my thing."

Rodger finished his salad, took a sip of wine, and replied, "I did look up some history on it in the U.S. Coast Pilot book I found on the shelf of books in the salon."

"Those were Clyde's books; I felt they belonged on the Sea Witch. What did it say about the Columbia River?"

"Let me serve the rest of the dinner, and I'll give you a narrative while we eat." Putting the empty salad plates on the tray, Rodger disappeared below deck. Reappearing with the gourmet hamburger patties, peas, and bread on two plates plus two glasses of Pinot Noir, he continued his narrative.

"The Pilot book says the Columbia River rises in British Columbia and flows for 360 miles before it enters the United States. It then flows southerly to the mouth of the Snake River; then westerly between Washington and Oregon where it empties into the Pacific Ocean."

"I'm impressed. How long is it in total if it's over 370 miles long before it leaves British Columbia?"

"It's over a thousand nautical miles long, and up to a mile wide as it goes through the Columbia River Gorge on its way to the Pacific Ocean. At the mouth of the river it's about five miles wide, if you include the marsh lands and low islands."

"Wow! That's some river. It must wind around a lot if it covers almost seven hundred hundred miles going through the state of Washington. If I remember correctly, Washington is only three hundred miles across."

"Some say the Columbia River is like a woman who keeps changing her mind, present company excluded of course, deciding on one direction and then another. According to the Pilot, it's navigable upstream for deep-draft ocean steamers as far as Portland and the Dalles. Light-draft steamers go farther, to Lewiston, Idaho."

"I had no idea it was that navigable. That would be an interesting boat trip in itself, wouldn't it?"

"Helen, you're not changing your mind about our trip to Tahiti, are you?"

"Of course not! By the way, the gourmet patty was delicious. I hate to break up this little interlude, but I suggest you close the dining room before it gets dark. I'll even have to sneak out on the dishes, as I need to continue tending the helm."

"I'll spring for your dishes tonight, then bring you coffee to keep you awake on the first watch. We should have a glorious sunset to share."

"Sounds great, Mate." Helen stood scanning their water path forward into the twilight of evening.

* * * *

"Here's your coffee, Skipper; it's robust and should help keep you awake. The sun has a ways to go before sunset, so while we wait for the big light show, explain how the auto-pilot works?" Rodger seated himself beside Helen enjoying the subtley difused light and shadow of the long twilight evening.

"It's not that complex, Rodg. Just pick your desired heading, hold the course for a few seconds, press the auto button, and release the helm. The autopilot takes over and becomes the helmsman; you are merely an observer. But, I might add, an important observer. You just don't have to have your hand on the tiller."

"That's all there is to it?"

"Yep, the autopilot will lock the course heading in memory, and will respond with helm corrections to keep that course."

"Amazing. It's probably more accurate than when we're holding a course."

"That's true; it doesn't get tired and it has an infinite attention span, which saves time and fuel, if you're under power."

"So what are the draw backs, besides not being able to shout *man overboard?*"

Helen, sipping her coffee and letting her mind skim back over the manual replied, "When it's difficult for us to steer manually, it's difficult for the auto pilot also. For example, when the helm is not balanced because of the wrong trim to the sails, or when the boat is yawing in a following sea, it's difficult steering for us and the auto pilot."

"Yawing in a following sea? That's a mouthful. What does that mean?"

"Remember a few days back when the wind came over our stern, and we seemed to be surfboarding when we sailed into Gray's Harbor? Do you also remember how the bow kept swinging off our heading, first one way, then the other? That's yawing in a following sea."

"I've got the picture. Anything else about the autopilot I should know?"

"Well, autopilots can't see, so they can't avoid obstacles or other vessels. That's why we must always maintain a watch."

"Darn, I was hoping this genie in a bottle would allow us to stay in bed while it tended the Sea Witch without our help."

Helen smiled. "You said you thought we should give our third crewmember a name. How about Genie? She is almost magic."

"Sounds good to me, but I didn't know a genie was a woman. I always thought of a genie as a man." Rodger sat on the gunnels and faced Helen even though her gaze was fixed forward.

"I guess it all depends on your point of view. Genie, for you, can be a man, for me it's a woman. Or we could compromise and declare that it is non-sexual and Genie is an it."

"I don't like that idea, but Genie does sound like a good name." Rodger replied shifting his gaze to the far horizon.

"So be it, Genie is bi-sexual. For you it's a man, for me it's a woman. How about a coffee refill with a jigger of Drambuie? After all, this is a celebration."

"What are we celebrating?" asked Rodger hopefully.

Helen smiled, but chose to ignore the inference. "The arrival and the naming of our third crew member, Genie, of course."

Taking her coffee mug, Rodger disappeared below. Helen sat at the tiller smiling as she relived their recent conversation and scanning the ocean waters ahead. The water was relatively flat except for the gentle rise and fall of rollers that reminded her of a children's roller coaster ride. She closed her eyes going inward. *This is turning out to be a wonderful trip, and Rodg is a great companion; he gets more attractive every day. Is it that I see him in a different light, or is it because his health is returning? He looks more like a sailor now with tanned skin, a sparkle in his eyes, and sun-faded clothes. Even his Greek fisherman's hat has a sweatband. Yep, I believe my first mate is a man with whom I could spend the rest of my life.*

Helen was snapped out of her reverie by hearing Rodger's reappearance on deck. "This ought to put starch in your legs Captain; I propose a toast."

"O.K. Mate, have at it."

"To Genie, welcome aboard the good ship Sea Witch. May you always be true to your task. With fair winds to our back, we three shall see Tahiti together."

"I'll drink to that. Now let's sit here at the helm and watch Genie do her job."

"Move over here Helen, we don't have to have the tiller between us now, as long as we have Genie doing his job."

They laughed and snuggling together as they watched the sun set over the Pacific Ocean. Dramatic brilliant shades of red steadily pushed the blue of the sky over the horizon. The radiant color emphasized the clouds, as the great fireball dropped over the edge of the ocean. It's fiery rays continued to slash at the encroaching dusk. The sky darkened steadily, its hues changing from light blue to deep purple until finally it gave way to night. In the distance, a lighthouse penetrated the darkness casting spears of light toward them at one-minute intervals.

"Magnificent," exclaimed Rodger at the beauty of the scene. They stood together arm in arm.

"Wasn't that sunset amazing? And it's all an illusion," Helen murmured softly.

"What do you mean an illusion? What illusion? Rodger asked, surprised at Helen's remark.

"The sunset." Helen turned to face Rodger, a smile wrinkling the corners of her mouth.

"The sunset? The sun did set," countered Rodger. "What's an illusion about that?"

"No, it didn't," replied Helen with a 'gotcha' tone to her voice.

"What do you mean it didn't? We just sat here and watched it set. Where's the illusion?"

"Rodger, Sweetie…I mean Mate. The earth is rotating on its axis and the sun is stationary. We are turning on our axis away from the sun, not vice versa."

"I'll be darned…that's right. I guess it is an illusion. However, most of the people of the world would say they saw the sun set; not that they saw the earth rotate on its axis away from the sun."

"No Rodg, you can join the rest of the world and say, 'let's watch the sunset'"

"You're always a teacher, Skipper. I guess it's time for me to get some bunk time, so I'll say goodnight, and expect you to awaken me at midnight. Do I get a good night kiss, or is that against the rules?"

"The Captain doesn't usually kiss the First Mate good night…but let's bend a rule. Goodnight love."

* * * *

Helen turned her attention to the sails and the instrumentation mounted in front of her as Rodger makes his way forward to the salon. Opening the divan he spread out the double sleeping bag, and after going through his nightly ritual, slipped into bed. Sleep didn't come immediately, he lets his mind wander back over the events of the day: *they ran the bar out of Gray's' Harbor, had seen a basking whale, had a wonderful day of sailing, a gormet meal, and watched a brilliant sunset.*

It seemed strange going to bed alone after sharing this bed with Helen these past few days. Too bad you can't park a sailboat like you do a car for the night. On the other hand it's nice to have the journey continue twenty-four hours a day. Perhaps we'll be able to average a hundred miles a day with good wind and favorable currents. At that rate we could be in San Diego in two weeks, counting an occasional day in port. Rodger finally succumbed to sleep as the steady, rhythmic splashing of waves on the hull created a lullaby known only to sailors.

Helen sat by the tiller for a long time watching the moon. *What a friendly companion the moon is..* The only other lights assuring her she was not alone were the shore lights, and the on-again, off-again beams of light from a lighthouse. The beacon light was coming from behind now. She pulled out the U.S. Coast Pilot to determine their position. *We spotted hundred-foot high Tillamook Rock just before sunset. It's lighthouse standing off the mainland by a strand of wash rocks is visible for eighteen miles. Since it's far behind us now, we're probably about fifteen miles south of it. Haystack Rock is coming up next,* it *should be easy to identify being* two *hundred and thirty five feet high. I guess we are about three miles off shore and the wind is holding steady at nine knots from the southwest and no known obstructions lay ahead of us.*

She listened to the autopilot making occasional corrections to the tiller. *Good old Genie,* she smiled. *How I love her.* It was time for Rodger's watch so Helen scanned the sea for obstacles such as floating logs or other boats. Satisfied all was clear, she went below and lit the oil stove to brew a fresh pot of coffee. When it started to perk, she awakened Rodger. "Rise and shine, Mate. There's hot coffee to awaken you and hopefully keep you awake for the next four hours."

"Is it really my watch already? I just closed my eyes." Rodger sat up in bed more asleep than awake.

"That was four hours ago, Mate." Helen gave him a friendly push causing him to fall back to his pillow. She leaned over and plantd a kiss on his mouth then withdrew before he could grab her.

Helen returned topside, while Rodger slid out of bed and dressed. After splashing cold water on his face, he filled two coffee mugs, grabbed his jacket, and ascended the stairs to the deck. Helen was leaning back in the cockpit staring at the top of the mast. Rodger followed her gaze. "What do you see up there, Skipper?"

"Just checking the wind direction by the weather vane. We're sailing about 30 degrees off the wind, on a broad reach, and the knot meter says we're making six knots. At this rate we should be in Newport by lunchtime tomorrow."

"I'm all for that; maybe then I can catch up on my sleep. Here's your cup of coffee, mind if I sit beside you while you drink it?" Helen asked in a sensual voice.

"I wouldn't have it any other way." Rodger put his arm around her shoulders, pulling her tight to him to share their body warmth.

"Where are we, approximately?" asked Rodger as he looked into the night sky.

"Do you see that foothill over there? It's about a thousand feet high, heavily wooded, and pitches abruptly to the sea ending in that rocky broken cliff."

"Yes, I see it."

"That's called Double Peak, and it puts us half way between Cape Falcon and Tillamook Head. The GPS tells us we have 68 nautical miles to go before we get to Newport."

Rodger tapped the GPS dial face gently. "The autopilot interfacing with the GPS sure relieves the tediousness of a long sail. Having it mounted out here on the cabin bulkhead is handy, but what about water damage in heavy weather?"

"I was going to talk to you about that when we make Newport. I think we should buy a dodger to protect it and us from heavy weather."

"A dodger? What's a dodger?"

"It's like a wrap around windshield with an arched canvas roof to fend off rain, wind, and bow spray. It'll protect Genie, and we can get under it too, since Genie has control of the the tiller."

"I'm liking Genie more all the time," Rodger said with wonder and amusement in his voice.

"It's your watch, Mate. If you see an obstacle, override the tiller and steer around it. If there's a drastic change in the weather, wake me so we can trim the sails, or do whatever has to be done. If it's only a moderate change, watch your tell-tales and trim the sails yourself. If you have a problem of any kind, awaken me. Now that my watch is over, I'll note in the ship's log the latitude and longitude, and our course. You do the same after your watch. I'm off to bed."

"Goodnight, Captain." Rodger zipped his jacket against the night air and settled down beside the tiller. The GPS told him the heading was one hundred eighty-five degrees, and with a nine-knot breeze out of the northwest, it should be a comfortable sail on a starboard reach. The degree of list registered thirty degrees and the tell-tails were parallel.

The night sky appeared dark, but not foreboding. Some stars shown through the low-level clouds but most were covered a good deal of the time. The temperature felt like the low fifties; the waves remained slow rollers, four or five feet high. Phosphorus in the water made the edges of the bow wake sparkle in the night. Occasionally a fish darting away from the hull became apparent as it left a trail of phosphorus similar to an airplane vapor trail in the sky.

Rodger threw the cold remains of his coffee over the side. Carefully checking the water path ahead for dead heads or other obstacles, he went below for a coffee refill. Helen was facing away from him on the divan; still he could hear her gentle rhythm of her breathing. Fighting his urge to slip into the bed beside her, he only smiled at the thought of holding her close as she slept looking so vulnerable. He poured a mug of coffee and threw in a shot of Drambui as a compensation for his unfulfilled desire. Climbing the five steps to the cockpit, he stood beside the tiller sipping his coffee and watching the night sky and the water path ahead. They were maintaining six knots and all was well.

It was four o'clock when Helen stuck her head out of the companionway. "Good morning," she called out.

Rodger, lost in his reverie, came to with a start. "Well, I was just about to go below and awaken you, but all these stars got in my eyes."

"I would like to think that you weren't asleep mate," said Helen testily. "That would be a Captain's Mast offense."

"That sounds pretty bad, whatever it is. No, I wasn't asleep, just day dreaming."

"What were you day dreaming about, Rodg?"

"I'll tell you after you tell me what a Captain's Mast is."

"A Captain's Mast is a trial before the Captain for the breach of a rule. Falling asleep on watch is very serious, especially in wartime."

"Believe me Helen, I wasn't asleep…are we at war?"

"If you say you were day dreaming, I believe you. That's the end of it," replied Helen testily.

"I'll take my day dream with me and go below, Captain. See you in the morning."

Helen scolded herself for being upset over the possibility that Rodger might be asleep. *I have to realize he's not used to being awake for four hours in the middle of the night. On the other hand, he has to realize how important it is that he stay alert for obstacles and wind change. Perhaps we should split the mid watch.*

* * * *

Chapter 17

▼

Seated at the Sea Witch's tiller, Helen watched the sunrise above the portside bow, splashing scattered clouds in vibrant shades of pink. *'Red in the morning, sailor takes warning,'* The old marine's omen came to her. *And that's exactly what I'm going to do, even though the weather conditions appear to be stable. The GPS tells me we're still fourteen miles from Newport, Oregon.*

In the far distance Helen could see the large concrete bridge arching the ocean entrance to Depot Bay. According to the Pilot Book, the bridge has a vertical clearance of forty-eight feet, but boats are cautioned against entering the bay at night, even though floodlights illuminate the bridge. Even so, Depot Bay is considered the best all-weather shelter for small boats on this stretch of the coast.

She momentarily wondered why she hadn't chosen that as their port-of call. Then remembered she'd chosen Newport instead of Depot Bay because Newport is a customs port of entry, thus making it a good place to stop on their journey south. Helen studied the coastal chart carefully, she knew the Yaquina Reef had to be carefully navigated. Being a half-mile off the entrance to Newport, it was a ridge of hard rock and sand with water depths of only five to thirteen feet. Runnign parallel to the shore for one and one half miles, the only opening to get to Newport is in the middle of the reef. This opening divides the reef making it two reefs. The north half being called Yaquina Reef; the south half is called South Reef. A bell buoy marks the southern end of Yaquina Reef.

As wind picked up the smooth rollers changed to a two-foot chop topped with whitecaps. Helen adjusted the sails, ratcheting down the jib, main, and mizzen sheets. The stronger winds with the sails close-hauled make the Sea Witch heel over to a 25-degree list. The hull speed increased to six knots. Helen put on her life jacket and banged on the cabin roof with her coffee cup.

After a couple of minutes Rodger thrust his head out of the companionway and surveyed the sky. "Do we have a problem skipper?"

"No, but I think you should be on deck, there's a small craft warning on the weather report. We'll be approaching Newport within an hour, and we have to find a buoy-marked channel. I've never been this far south, so it's all new to me. Put on your life jacket as things could get exciting."

Rodger appeared on deck fully dressed including his life jacket. "Do you want a cup of coffee and breakfast?"

"Sounds good to me, Mate, but let me fix it. You take the helm. I'm stiff from sitting with Genie."

Rodger came aft and wrapped his arms around her. "You look like you need a little tender loving care."

"You're right, Rodg, I do; I'm not used to lonely, four-hour watches. However, we'll get used to it, I'm told."

"Go below and lie down for awhile. I'll call you if I need a hand. It'll be an hour before we have to be on the lookout for the marker buoy."

"You're thoughtful, Rodg, I didn't realize how tired I was." Said Helen leaning into Rodger's embrace. "I apologize for being short with you last night. I thought you weren't completely awake and in control of the helm."

"Apology accepted, Skipper. Sometimes my medication makes me look a little spacey."

"Is the cold night air giving your lungs trouble?" Helen drew away and started for the companionway down to the cabin interior.

"Only when I breathe." Rodger expected a reply to his attempted humor, but got none.

Going below, Helen slipped off her deck shoes and stretched out on the bed Rodger had just vacated. Rollling over in a state of fatique, she buried her face into his pillow. His scent was still there causing her to smile to herself and drift off to sleep.

Rodger studied the GPS confirming they were still an hour north of the bell buoy they sought. *The sky's clear, so I shouldn't have trouble finding the buoy. The change in the weather might just make our journey more exciting. I'm feeling more comfortable sailing the Sea Witch now, I guess I'm learning to be a seaman. In fact, I could probably handle the Sea Witch by myself if need be. However, it would be a lonely trip without Helen. She's wonderful! I got lucky when I chose to buy her boat. I'd still be in Poverty Bay trying to learn how to sail.*

Rodger snuggled down inside his jacket to get more out of the weather when a sudden fit of coughing doubled him over. He tried desperately to control it, because he knew it enflamed his throat lining to the point of closing it. Forcing himself to take a series of shallow breaths, he regained control of his breathing. Wiping the tears from his eyes, he sank back exhausted. *I'd better get myself to a doctor in Newport for a check up.* He slipped a pill into his mouth and quickly washed it down with a swallow of luke-warm coffee.

Even though the waves were building, he was able to make out the marker buoy he was looking for when it was still a half-mile away. Pulling out the coastal chart, he studied it carefully. *I know I have to make a ninety-degree turn after I reach the buoy. I need to slacken the sails to spill some of the air before I make my turn, as I'll have both wind and sea on my beam. This could be courting a knock down, but I think I can do this, with Genie at the helm. Good old genie, I'll let Helen sleep.*

Once he'd slackened the mizzen and mainsheet; Rodger moved aside to slacken the jib sheet, in order to spill a third of the air from the sails. The hull slowly righted itself from twenty-five to ten degrees. After passing the South Reef buoy he momentarily overrode Genie and slowly brought the bow around to port. Quickly determining the new compass setting for the GPS, he adjusted the jib, main, and mizzen sheets until the tell-tells were parallel. The hull speed dropped to four knots. They were now a half-mile from the entrance to Newport harbor. Rodger sat back and smiled to himself, *I'll bet Helen will be proud of my seamanship.*

As the Sea Witch came within three hundred yards of the bridge, Rodger made a fist and rapped his knuckles on the cabin roof. Helen thrust her head out of the hatch opening and quickly took account of their position. "You made that turn in these winds without calling me?"

"Yeah, Skipper," surprised at her obvious agitation. "I thought I'd do it and let you sleep."

"Not smart, Rodger. We could easily have had a knockdown. One rogue wave or wind gust would do it."

"Okay, I guess I wanted to show you, and myself, I could handle the Sea Witch even under heavy weather conditions. You didn't say you wanted me to awaken you before we made the turn."

"You're right, she realized, I didn't. I just assumed you'd call me and we would do it together, with me at the helm. Obviously, you knew what to do, and you did it. Congratulations are in order, I guess. But next time, I'd like to be awake."

"Thanks Skipper, as I've said before, I've had a good teacher." Rodger was relieved at the Helen's return to a more pleasant attitude as she took over the helm.

"Drop the sails and flake the mizzen and main on their booms, Mate. Stow the jib in its sail bag and leave it connected to the forestay. Then crank up the engine and we'll come in under power. We probably won't be in Newport more than a day, unless we decide to have a dodger installed." Helen's orders were delivered in the once again crisp, authoritative voice of a ship's captain.

After starting the engine, Rodger returned to the cockpit to watch their entrance into Newport. "I like the idea of a dodger. It would be good to have a windshield with a roof for protection from the elements. It's a long way to Tahiti, any protection we can get sounds like money well spent."

Helen stood at the helm scanning the approach into Newport. "I'm sure we'll find a shop near the marina that does canvas work. I traveled by car through Newport once and it has a well-protected harbor. Actually, it's a typical seaport town, where life is dictated by the tides and weather. The depletion of native salmon forced the town to cater more to tourists. It has a coastal ocean beauty to attract travelers, and people like to go out on the ocean, even if they don't have fishing as an excuse."

Rodger settled into the cockpit seat opposite Helen. "If it isn't a working port, is tourism driving the local economy?"

"It's both. There still are some salmon and other kinds of fish and sea life. You'll see trollers, crabbers, long-liners, shrimpers, draggers, charterboats, and pleasure craft." Helen corrected the positon of the bow to line up with the bridge archway they would go under and into the large, protective bay of Newport.

"Hold it! I know about charterboats and pleasure craft, but what is a troller, a long-liner, a shrimper, and a dragger?" Rodger stood at the gunnels surveying the approaching entranceway.

"A troller is a commercial fishing boat with two tall trolling poles. The poles drop down to a thirty-degree angle off the water when they are fishing and two steel lines go down from each pole. Each line has six lures or spreads attached at one fathom intervals starting from the bottom. Therefore, they pull twenty-four lures through the water at one time.

A long-liner fishes for halibut by putting hooks on a long line that lies on or close to the bottom where the halibut congregate. Some lines are a mile long with a thousand hooks. A shrimper drags a sock-like net behind searching out schools of shrimp in order to scoop them up in the sock. A dragger is used to harvest salmon, sea bass, or mackerel and has a drag net also like a shrimper only the net has a much larger mesh. That's about as much as I know about commercial fishing."

"I'm surprised you know that much." Rodger stood to watch the scene before them. The bridge that was a part of the coast highway loomed high above them. Other boats were coming and going and a festive tourist crowd lined the railing of the bridge above them to get a better view of all the water activity including the line of boats like a water highway.

"Clyde used to point out the different work boats and tell me how they fished. He had a wealth of information about the sea and those who made a living from it."

"Has this trip helped you in your transition to life without Clyde?"

"Yes. However, I will always cherish the ten years Clyde and I had together."

"That's the way it should be. We are capable of loving more than one person in our lifetime as a primary partner; each partner will always be a part of us. We are the sum total of all our life experiences. How about you? Do you miss Irene and your sons?"

"I think of them daily, and I know that they will always be a part of my life." Rodger paused as Newport Bridge loomed overhead. "Incidentally, that bridge we are about to go under is spectacular. It seems strange to be going on the other side of the coast highway, but it certainly will give us a safe, sheltered moorage. Look up there at people that are waving to us, they probably wish they were down here."

"Yes," said Helen. "I'm sure we make an enviable picture sailing in from the ocean on the Sea Witch. Look to port along the bank; see those women working at those two fish cleaning tables."

"They really are skillfull at cleaning those salmon for the sporting fishermen. I guess there are still some salmon left and men don't always like to clean their own fish, do they?"

"You got it, and those sea birds are loving the scraps being thrown to them. Did you ever hear such a cacophony of sound?" A yawn interrupted Rodger's observations. "Right now I could sure use some sleep."

"An hour from now we can go to bed; in the meantime we have docking and registering to do."

"Aye aye, Captain. I can hardly wait."

*   *   *   *

CHAPTER 18

▼

The Sea Witch rocked gently at its mooring as the September sun cast its rays from directly overhead filling the salon with light. The first thing Rodger saw as he opened his eyes was the gimbaled lamp above him, swinging gently back and forth to the rhythm of wavelets, rocking the hull. Rolling out of bed Rodger glanced toward the clock fitted into the bulkhead across from him. "Good Grief, it's 12:15. We've slept half of the day away."

Helen stirred. "So? We needed sleep after our two-day sail from Westport. Do you have something more important you wanted to do today?" Helen propped herself up on one elbow, face still full of sleep and one eye open.

"Yes," replied Rodger as he sat waking up on the side of the bed. "We need to find someone to make a dodger. But first, I vote for locating a good restaurant for breakfast."

"Now you're talking. I'll grab my things and head for the shower while you make the coffee. Helen swung her legs over the edge of the divan, her feet resting on the floor beside Rodger's. Leaning her sleep-flushed body against his, she teasingly tangled her fingers into his hair. "By the way," she murmured. "Last night was another stroll to the mountain top and a nice stroll down the other side."

"For me too, love. Now, go shower before you start something we shouldn't take time for right now. I'll make the coffee. Better make that a cold shower."

Helen gave his hair a playful tug then. Pulling on her jeans and a tee shirt, she grabbed her toiletries and bounded up the salon steps. Then pausing at the top, "Spoilsport" she taunted over her shoulder before disappearing onto the deck.

Falling backwards on the bed, Rodger closed his eyes savoring for a moment longer its heady memories of the preceding night. He was reluctant to leave this haven where they had satisfied their love for one another. *Wow! She's something.* Finally, with a sigh, he rose, and slipping into his cloths, lit the oil cook stove for coffee making.

While it perked, Rodger stepped on deck to survey their surroundings. The harbor was well protected from the ocean. In fact, he couldn't see the ocean. The raised highway that formed the land-locked harbor ran between the bay and the ocean. The picturesque arched bridge, under which they had sailed yesterday, was the only access to or from the ocean. The bay, which was also the mouth of the Yaquina River, had extensive mud flats visible as the tide was out.

"Hi there mate; where are you headed?"

Rodger turned to the direction of the voice. The inquirer, a middle-aged man, his darkly tanned skin, sun bleached hair, and clothing gave him the look of a mariner.

"We're bound for Tahiti." Rodger replied moving closer to his visitor.

"No kidding!" Rodger's visitor rested one foot on the gunnels of the Sea Witch. "That's quite a distance. I was in Tahiti back in '83. You look like you have a boat that's up to the job, a Tahiti ketch, haven't seen one in years. He leaned forward extending his hand, "I'm Dorm Stillwell."

Rodger gripped the proffered hand, "I'm Rodger McCauley." he responded. "We left Des Moines, Washington three weeks ago," he went on to explain, "but we've had several delays enroute; we're not really on a tight schedule."

Dorm laughed, "If it's taken you three weeks to go four hundred miles, I guess you aren't on a tight schedule." Dorm was a tall, handome man in his forties, pleasant to talk to.

"I think we've resolved our problems," said Rodger still standing on the gunnels. "The boat is nearly ready for the rest of the trip."

"What do you have left to do?" Asked Dorm's, his eyes sweeping the Sea Witch from stem to stern.

"We thought we'd find a sail maker and have a dodger made. We have added equipment we'd like to protect."

"There are several canvas shops in Newport and they're all good, but the closest one is in that large van-like truck in the parking lot." Dorm stepped back on the dock and pointed to the far side of the marina parking lot. "Charlie can usually finish and install a dodger in one day."

"That sounds like what I'm looking for. We're anxious to get farther south before the weather turns on us."

"You said we, you have a shipmate?"

"My Skipper is in the showers, she should be along any minute," Rodger replied matter-of-factly.

Dorm's eyes widened. "You have a woman Skipper?"

Rodger laughed at Dorm's surprise, "She's the former owner and she's teach me how to sail it."

"You're not a sailor and your going to sail to Tahiti with a woman in command?" Dorm's smile had turned to a look of disbelief.

"Yep," Rodger's voice took on a hint of defensiveness. "She knows enough for both of us, and I'm a good learner."

"Well, good luck, Rodger. You're probably going to need it." Dorm walked away slowly shaking his head from side-to-side.

* * * *

Rodger was sitting on the cabin roof enjoying his first cup of coffee when Helen arrived fresh from the shower. Her face shone with delight as she approached the Sea Witch. "I recommend the showers; I'll hold down the fort while you take yours."

"Good. I just talked to a guy who said the closest sail maker was doing business out of that van over there in the parking lot. I'll stop on my way to the showers and see if he can do it today. If he can, I'll send him over."

"Good! I'll spruce up the cabin while you're gone. Then, I'm up for breakfast."

Rodger grabbed his toilet articles and headed across the parking lot looking for some sign of life from the van. "Ahoy, any one there?"

"What can I do for you?" a voice boomed from the depth of the van.

Rodger peered in to the dim interior. At the far end of the van a hulk of a man sat at a sewing machine, his beachwear of shorts and black tank top exposed muscular brown arms and legs, both generously adorned with numerous, well-done tattoos. A salt-and-pepper ponytail, hanging to the middle of his back, was held in place by a tooled, leather band. "Do you make dodgers for sailboats?" Rodger inquired.

"You bet I do," replied the sailmaker as he walked to the opening of the van. "How soon do you need it?"

"Today, if possible." Rodger stood looking up into the van and at the man.

The man stepped down from the van and still towered over Rodger. "Tell me where you're moored, if I see your layout I can tell you if I can get it done today. It depends on the metal framework; the canvas and Plexiglas are the easy part."

"We're in slip A-15. I'm on my way to the showers, but my Skipper is aboard. She's expecting you." The sailmaker's eyes widened as he realized the skipper was a woman, but he said nothing.

Rodger showered and returned to the Sea Witch just as the sail maker was finishing up the measuring. Helen sat near the tiller watching the procedure as Rodger called out, "I see you found us. What do you think; can you do it today?"

"Yep, it's do-able. What color do you want: Red, blue, tan, or white?"

"What do you think, Helen?" Rodger looked over at Helen expecting an answer.

"White will match the rest of our canvas," she replied light heartedly.

"Then white it is. How much to do the job?" Rodger looked directly at the sailmaker knowing the dodger was a done deal regardless of the price. Rodger wasn't in a shopping or bargaining mood, he was ready for breakfast.

"Two-hundred-seventy-five dollars should cover it."

"Sounds like a deal. We need to find a restaurant, any suggestions?"

"Well, I like Mo's up on Bay Street. The sailmaker jerked his head over a brawny left shoulder. Tell them Charlie sent you, and they'll treat you right."

"Thanks, Charlie. By the way, this is Helen, I'm Rodger."

"Pleased to meet you." He dipped his chin in acknowlegement, the long ponytail bobbing with each nod of his head. "I should have your job done by the end of the day."

Following Charlie's direction they headed toward Mo's restaurant. "Wow! Helen exclaimed squeezing Rodger's hand. "What a hunk, and I don't mean handsome."

"He's big all right, and if the tattoos are any indication, he's probably a sailor. It shouldn't surprise us if most of the people we run into in a marina are sailors...or ustabes...or wannabes."

Moe's restaurant was a good choice. Strolling the main street of Newport after breakfast they paused beside a large bronze-plated monument inscribed with the names of locals who had gone out into the Pacific Ocean and never returned. Rodger sensed a slight quickening in Helen's breathing, taking her her hand in his, he turned to face her. "Look Helen, if you're having any second thoughts about this trip, now is the time to say so. We don't have to do it, you know. All fantasies aren't fulfilled."

"I know that, Rodg. Sometimes, I do have second thoughts she admitted, but then I quote Helen Keller to myself, 'all life should be an adventure,' and I believe that. She smiled up into Rodger's face then, impulsively, she flung her arms around his neck, and planted a hard and passionate upon his lips.

Taken by surprise, it took Rodger a moment to catch his breath. He quickly wrapped his arms around Helen and drew her close. "I agree about all life being an adventure, and thanks for the encouragement," he whispered into her hair. "All life should be an adventure, and with you it definitely is."

"I've decided to see a doctor while we're here and have an x-ray." He stepped back from Helen, his hands resting on her shoulders, "I'd like to know if I'm holding my own."

"How do you think you're doing?" A frown of concern creased her forehead.

"Most of the time I feel like I'm doing better than okay. Only once in awhile, after a coughing bout, I wonder."

"I saw a clinic near the restaurant," Helen remembered. "Let's see if we can get a doctor to look at you."

"Okay, we might as well get this over with," Rodger sighed. "Do you want to go with me or do you want to be a tourist and shop for that gypsy negligee?" he added with a chuckle.

"Of course, I want to go with you. The negligee can wait…can't it?" quipped Helen, buying into innuendo. "We're in this together, remember? And I don't mean the negligee."

Hand-in-hand Rodger and Helen entered the clinic. Dr. Barklay greeted them, a middle-aged man with a Scottish look about him and a slight accent in his speech pattern. He listened carefully while Rodger described his illness and the reason for his visit to the clinic. After hearing the state of their transiency, Dr. Barklay agreed to work Rodger into his schedule. Partly to accommodate Rodger, he admitted, and partly because it wasn't everyday he ran into a diagnosed case of Tuberculosis.

After examining Rodger, he ordered x-rays to be taken. Once the technician delivered the x-rays, Doctor Barklay invited Helen to join them in his office. "Your's is an interesting case, Rodger. I don't have your last x-rays to compare these with, but I see scarring on your lung walls, which is a sign of healing. Unless I miss my guess, I would say you're doing better than just holding your own. However, I think we should also have Helen x-rayed. This is communicable and you are living in close quarters."

Rodger exploded from his chair. "Oh dear Lord. If I've infected you, Helen, I'll never forgive myself."

"Easy, Rodg," Helen soothed, pulling Rodger back down beside her. "He only wants to x-ray me. If I am infected, well then, I've always known being with you was a risk, a calculated risk. I factored that risk in right from the beginning."

Rodger clung to Helen's hand, his face contorted with dispair. "My doctor told me I wasn't contagious once I started taking my medication,"he insisted.

Dr Barklay rose from his chair. If you'll come with me, Helen, I'll take you to x-ray. My technician is expecting you."

Helen followed Dr. Barklay from the room. The door closed behind them, leaving Rodger alone. He dropped his head into his hands. "Oh, dear God," he moaned. "What have I done?"

It was only a matter of moments before Doctor Barklay re-entered his office, seating himself across from Rodger. "I guess you know having Tuberculosis is a serious condition, and you tell me you're sailing to Tahiti? I wonder if that is the smart thing to be doing in your condition?"

"Look Doctor, that's the whole point." Rodger's voice trembled as he struggled to control his emotions. "I was given less than a year to live, this trip was something I've always wanted to do, and time, obviously, is of the essence."

"I get the impression you two haven't known each other very long. Are you married, or is that any of my business?" Dr Barklay sat back in his chair inviting conversation.

"No, we are not married, but we are intimate. I trusted my doctor's diagagnosis."

"Helen didn't necessarily get this from you, although, if she tests positive, in all probability, she did."

"What do you mean, she might not have gotten it from me?" Rodger stared in disbelieve at the doctor.

"One third of the world has been expose to this disease. Some authorities feel each of us have a spot of something in us just waiting to become active when the time is right."

"That's a very disturbing thought, doctor." Rodger squirmed in his chair uncomfortably.

Helen and the technician re-entered the office that moment, interrupting their conversation. Accepting the x-rays from the tchnician, Dr Barklay stood andplaced them onto the light window, studying them intently. Then, "Helen, you have the early stages of tuberculosis...but," he hastened, "let me explain what that means."

"Oh God," Rodger swept Helen into his arms. "How could I have done this to you?"

Helen shuddered, surrendering for a moment, to the warmth and support of Rodger's body as she tried to assimilate what the doctor had said, what Rodger was saying. Slipping out of Rodger's embrace, she sank quickly in a nearby chair. She glanced first towards the doctor and then at Rodger, a sad smile replaced her look of bewilderment. "We really are in this together aren't we love?"

Rodger gripped the back of her chair. "I never should have trusted my doctor's diagnosis," he fumed. "What can be done for Helen, Doctor?"

Moving to her side, Dr. Barklay took Helen's hand gently in his own. "This isn't the end of the world. We've detected this early on, and with today's advanced medicines, your chances of a full recovery are excellent." He turned to Rodger, "However, you'll need to hold up on the trip a few days. I need to prescribe medicine for Helen and have her around for at least three days to see how she responds. We can start treatment today."

The room was silent as the three exchanged glances, each trying to read one another's thoughts. Rodger was the first to speak. "We'll do whatever is best for Helen; the trip can wait."

Helen rose from her chair and crossing over to Rodger, took his hand, her eyes searching deeply into his. "We'll do what the doctor says Rodg, but the trip doesn't have to be put off for very long. I have a healthy constitution. I'm sure I can beat this thing."

"You're so brave, Helen. You know what T.B. can do to a person by looking at me."

"I've been looking at you for a month, and I'm in love with you." She turned back to Dr. Barklay. "Give me the prescriptions doctor; I want to go back to the Sea Witch and lie down. This has turned out to be a fatiguing day after all."

"Keep in mind that you will be contagious until the medication takes effect." Dr. Barklay advised. "That is another reason I want you here. Stay away from people until you come back to see me in three days. I could have you hospitalized, but, if you'll quarantine yourself on your boat, that will be sufficient. Just stay away from everyone, except Rodger," he cautioned.

The doctor left the room returning with two prescription bottles. Helen fought to regain her composure, while Rodger held her. The doctor said, "This is Isoniazid and Pyrazinamide. Take it according to the directions on the bottles. Here are some up-to-date brochures concerning tuberculosis and an explanation of the medicines I have perscribed."

Helen, regaining her composure, exclaimed, "I had no idea tuberculosis was so prevalent in the world, nor so easily cured, if caught in time. Did you know that, Rodger?" She made no move to leave the comforting circle of Rodger's arms.

"I knew there are a lot of us with tuberculosis," Rodger replied, "but I had no idea it was so common. It used to be called consumption, I'm told." Rodger took Helen by the hand to leave. "I just wish I'd been diagnosed sooner." He dropped his arm to Helen's waist. "We'll get back to the Sea Witch now and we'll follow your directions, Doctor. Is it okay to walk to the marina or should we take a taxi cab?"

"It's only three blocks," replied the doctor. "Walk if you'd like, just avoid close contact with people. They won't get infected by touching you or things that you have touched. It's enough if you just stay away from people."

Helen held out her hand to the doctor. "Thanks for picking up on this; I'll try to be a good patient." She added brightly as she looked up at Rodger. "Rodg, and I will see this through."

"Right Helen, we'll see it through together. From now on, or at least for awhile, I'll not only be your deck hand, but your nurse."

"O.K. nurse, let's get back to the Sea Witch. I need some T.L.C."

"Really?" replied Rodger.

* * * *

Chapter 19

▼

Awakening early the next morning Rodger lay silently beside Helen listening to her rhythmic breathing. Carefully, so as not to disturb her, he slid one leg over the edge of the bed. Helen stirred. "Good morning love," she murmured. "Don't get up, I want to talk to you."

"What do you want to talk about?" Rodger asked knowing it would have to do with her health.

"I want to know about tuberculosis. I know what the doctor said, but you have the disease, so what didn't he tell me?"

Rodger rolled up on one elbow to face Helen. "I've learned there are ten to fifteen million Americans infected, but only ten percent will get sick from it. Unfortunately, you and I are in that ten percent group. Being detected early, you'll get well as long as you take your medicine. On the other hand, I may, or may not, beat this thing, according to what Dr. Barclay said yesterday. That's better news than what I've been living with the past few months."

Helen rolled on her side facing Rodger. "How come we don't hear about tuberculosis? I thought it was a thing of the past, like polio."

"Unfortunately, after thirty years of decline, T.B. is on the increase in the United States and around the world. In 1993 the World Health Organization declared tuberculosis as a global emergency because it claims more lives than any other infectious disease."

"Just our luck," sighed Helen. "How come Dr. Barclay said I might not have gotten it from you?"

"According to what I've read, a healthy adult, being exposed for twenty four hours a day to a contagious carrier has a 50% chance of getting it. The contagious carrier didn't have to be me, but it probably was. I hate the thought that I could have been the one who infected you. It just so happens, I had an advanced case before I knew what was wrong with me. I've always hated going to doctors and I kept putting it off, but I couldn't get rid of my cough. It wasn't until I started spitting up blood that I went to see Doctor Smith in Bellevue."

Helen pushed Rodger back on the bed and rolled over on him. Gently she placed a kiss on each eyelid, the tip of his nose, and his mouth. "Don't be too hard on yourself, Rodg, The fact is, I have it, and I'll do what ever is necessary to get rid of it."

Rodger wrapped his arms around her pulling her body down firmly upon his. "The doctor said he wants to see you in three days. If the medicine does its job, you'll not be contagious to anyone, according to him. I'll get up now, if you'll let me, and fix breakfast so you can take your medicine."

"Did I ever tell you that you're a spoilsport?"

Rodger laughed. "Under different circumstances, believe me, I wouldn't be." Rodger kissed her softly and extracting himself from their embrace stated, "It's amazing, that Dr. Barclay's pharmacist said thirty dollars worth of medicine will not only control tuberculosis, but will usually cure it. Unfortunately, not everyone in the world who has been infected with T.B. has thirty dollars for the medicine."

"That is sad isn't it? However, I have thirty dollars, so let's get on with our lives. I'll have eggs, bacon, hash-browns, and toast, if you please."

"That's my Skipper. In the meantime, lie there and enjoy your forced convalescence."

"Ugh! I just realized I can't leave the boat to even take a shower. This isn't going to be much fun."

"It beats being in isolation in a hospital room, and I'll serve you better food. I'll put on the coffee and head for the showers via the sailmaker's van. He'll be wondering why we didn't show up yesterday for the dodger," said Rodger. "Then, I'll fix breakfast."

"Okay Mate, I'll just lie here like a slug and read until breakfast is ready."

Rodger gathered fresh clothing, his shaving kit, and headed for the van. Boaters, taking advantage of the unusually warm days for early September, crowded the marina making the most of the summer weather. At full tide, with some boaters going out to cruise on the ocean and others going up the Yaquina for a day on the river, the bay bustled with activity.

The van sat in its usual place on the far side of the parking lot with a large sign on its side that read, *Charlie's Sails and Accessories*. Rodger walked around to the back of the van and called, "Ahoy there."

An angry voice boomed from the van's interior. "What happened to your need for a rush order on the dodger? It was ready for you yesterday afternoon."

"We had an unexpected change of plans," Rodger explained. "Helen was told by a doctor to go to bed for three days."

Charie's head appeared lthrough the open van door. "Nothing serious, I hope," the anger dissipating from his voice.

Avoiding the truth, Rodger replied, "No, she just needs to rest for a few days before we continue our trip to Tahiti."

"Tahiti is it? I spent a week in jail there once, back in my misspent, younger days. Nothing serious, just a typical bar fight." Charlie left his sewing machine and stood at the opening of the van looking down.

"Were you a sailor in the Navy, or a civilian sailor?" Rodger asked, relieved at Charlies change of attitude.

"I've been both, but at that time I was a civilian crewing out on a sixty-three footer out of New York. If I'd been in the Navy, the shore patrol would have sprung me out of the local jail in no time. Of course, they would have put me in the brig aboard ship. It's still confinement, but the food is a hell of a lot better, and the company is more selective."

Rodger turned to leave, "I'm on my way to the showers; I can pay you now and pick up the dodger on the way back to the Sea Witch."

Charlie stepped out of his van. onto the asphalt of the parking lot. "I'll carry it to your boat while you shower. I can just hang around there until you get back, you can pay me then."

"Well, O.K, but don't disturb Helen, she's sleeping."

"No problem." Charlie chuckled at the apprehension he sensed in Rodger's voice.

Rodger quickened his stride as he walked to the shower area. He liked Charlie, but he didn't totally trust a guy with all those tattoos and a ponytail, and for sure, one who had been in jail in Tahiti. Rodger showered, but didn't linger. Dressing quickly, he finished with his toiletries in record time. As he neared the Sea Witch, he saw Charlie sitting on the rail near the cockpit smoking a cigarette and apparently enjoying the beauty of the day.

"Hi Skipper," he called out as Rodger approached.

"You beat me here. I appreciate your delivery of the dodger, but I didn't mean to interrupt your work this long."

"I needed a break from my van, especially on such a beautiful day. I haven't heard anything from below, so I guess your lady is still sleeping. Charlie slipped from the railing and stooped to pick up a box and the dodger lying at his feet. I brought along tools needed to install the dodger in case you want me to do it. I work cheap on a day like this, if it were raining, the price would be higher."

Rodger laughed. "How much is cheap, Charlie?"

"Twenty five dollars would bring your tab up to an even three hundred dollars."

"You're hired. What about tax?"

"Not in Oregon. We pay a state income tax, but no sales tax." Charlie moved the dodger parts aboard as he spoke.

"That sounds good for the out-of-state tourists. How do you feel about it, Charlie?"

"I don't have a big income, so it's better for me." He than moved his toolbox closer to the job.

Helen stuck her head out of the hatch opening and surveyed the scene before her. "How can a lady sleep when there is all this talk going on outside her bedroom?"

"Sorry Skipper. Charlie's here with the dodger, he'll install it while I fix brunch."

"All right, I'll go back and lie down."

"You call her Skipper?"

"Do I have to go through this with you, too? Dorm Stillwell had the same question yesterday. What's with you guys? Haven't you ever heard of a woman skipper before?"

Charlie stopped working and faced Rodger. "Well, for sure it would be a problem for Dorm. He hates women. Now me, I love women. I only have trouble with it because skippering a sailboat requires a lot of knowledge and some strength."

Rodger grinned, "Helen has both, believe me."

"Okay, you ought to know," replied Charlie returning to his work. "It's just that we haven't had many women skippers around here. I might go back to sea myself, if I could find a woman like that."

Rodger went below to fix breakfast while Charlie continued installing the dodger. He expected to see Helen in bed, not sitting on the divan. "You're supposed to be in bed."

"I'm tired of the bed and it feels good to be up and clean after my sponge bath. Now, what do I do for the rest of the day?"

"Stay quiet and after breakfast go back to your reading. Dr. Barclay says rest is very important at this stage of the game."

Helen busied herself setting the table while Rodger made breakfast. "I wonder what he meant, Rodg, when he said some authorities think each of us has a spot, or flaw, in us that could do us in, if conditions were right?"

"We'll ask him about that when we see him day after tomorrow. By the way, I didn't see you take your pills. Did you?"

"O.K. Nurse, I'll take my pills if you'll give me a hug. I feel a need for some more tender loving care."

Rodger wrapped his arms around Helen and held her tight, thrilling as her body pulsated against his. Gently pushing her head back, he kissed her firmly, but lovingly upon the lips.

"Hey you two," Charlie yelled down the open hatch. "I'm outta here."

Rodger helped Helen settle back on the divan and then went topside to pay Charlie. After a quick inspection, he turned to the sailmaker, "The dodger looks good. I'm sure there'll be times when we'll really appreciate the protection it'll give us. Here's your money and thanks for the rush job, even though, as it worked out, we didn't need a rush job."

"Okay Skipper,...er, I mean Mate." Charlie shook his head and grinned. "No sir, I never did see a skipper like her."

* * * *

Chapter 20

Rodger called a taxi to take them to their appointment with Dr. Barclay. The receptionist, who hadn't been their on their first visit, greeted, then escorted them to the doctor's private office. Dr. Barclay stood as they entered. "It's good to see you looking so well, Helen. Rodger must be a good nurse."

"He is a good nurse."

Dr. Barclay continued, "I'll need to have some blood work done and an x-ray before we can say for sure the treatment is effective. He paged his nurse on the intercom, "Mary, would you take care of Helen's testing and x-ray? Helen, come back as soon as Mary is through with you. He turned to Rodger, "You and I will have to wait here for the results."

Once Mary escorted Helen from the office, Dr. Barclay sat back in his chair interweaving his hands behind his head. He signaled Rodger with a nod to have a seat opposite him. "So, you two are headed for Tahiti. Sounds like a wonderful adventure. Have you made any other trips like this?"

"This will be a first," replied Rodger rising restlessly getting to his feet. "Helen is the Skipper, and I am the Mate. She and her deceased husband sailed for ten years around the Northwest before I bought the boat from her," he explained. As I told you, I wanted to satisfy a long held fantasy of sailing to Tahiti. When Helen discovered I wasn't much of a sailor, she offered to skipper the boat for me." Rodger was beginning to feel uncomfortable as the doctor continued his questioning.

Dr. Barkley continued to lean back in his chair even though Rodger had chosen to pace the floor. "Really! How big is this sailboat?"

"It's a thirty foot Tahiti Ketch, but it has the latest instrumentation," replied Rodger defensively and shifting nervously from one foot to the other, anxious to hear the results of Helen's testing.

"Thirty feet. That's not very big for such a long, ocean-crossing. However, smaller boats have done it." He paused. "I just hope Helen is going to be strong enough for the trip. Her cure requires not only medication, but also moderate activity."

"We're both going to be disappointed if we have to postpone this trip. However, you're the doctor; we'll let you tell us what is possible. Then in an attempt to reduce the tension that had been building, he asked, "Incidently Dr. Barklay, the other day you made a statement that puzzled us. You said some authorities think that within each of us is a spot or a flaw that could bring about our demise."

"That's the theory," replied Dr. Barklay mentally shifting to this new subject. "And I believe it that within every person there is a weak spot or flaw, which could be his or her undoing. I probably shouldn't have mentioned it, as it's only a theory. However, it doesn't just pertain to physical health, but can include mental health as well," he continued warming up to the subject.

I first read about this in the writings of the Scottish New Testament Interpreter, William Barclay," he smiled. "I would like to think he was a relative of mine, but I don't know that. Anyway, he was talking about temptation, which of course, is usually a mental thing. He says temptation, such as is common to man, comes not only from outside us, it also comes from inside us. He says if there were nothing in us to which temptation could appeal, it would be helpless to defeat us." The doctor continued his comfortable laid backposition in his chair. "He concludes by saying that in every one of us there is a weak spot or flaw; and at that spot temptation launches its attack."

"Really! Are you saying that we all have a predisposition to some flaw of character or a physical flaw, or both."

"Yes. But can I prove it? No."

"Well, it's something to think about." *Where is he going with this?* Rodger wondered uneasily?

"Yes, it is…isn't it." Dr. Barklay stood as he heard footsteps approaching from the hallway.

Helen and Mary entered the room bringing an end to the unusual conversation. Mary handed the doctor two documents and left. Dr. Barklay glanced over the page then turned to Helen. "Good news! The medication is effective. You should be able to continue your adventure, as long as Rodger does the heavy work for awhile."

Rodger gave Helen a hug, both breathing an audible sigh of relief. Rodger grinned at Helen, "We'll leave tomorrow, if that's O.K. with you Captain?"

"Based on what Dr. Barclay said, I guess I should turn the command over to you, Rodg. You've been a good student, I think you can sail the Sea Witch even without me, if you have to."

Stepping back Rodger took Helen's hand in his, "Probably so," he whispered, "but I don't want to ever sail her without you. As far as I'm concerned, you will always be my captain."

"Then your captain says, we sail at morning slack tide, weather permitting."

"Aye, Aye Captain," replied Rodger smiling.

* * * *

Chapter 21

Rodger opened his eyes to find Helen smiling down at him. "O.K. sleepy head," she scolded, "it's time to hit the deck."

"What time is it?" Rodger muttered into his pillow.

Six-thirty and slack tide is at eight o'clock." Helen ignored Rodger's groan. "We'll have to scramble to catch it as it only lasts an hour."

"What's so critical about slack tide?" Rodger yawned, still groggy from sleep.

"Did you notice the water conditions under the bridge when we came in?" Helen persisted.

"Yes," he admitted. I remember it was turbulent, and the tide pushed us in at quite a clip."

"That's what we don't want going out. If we can't have it going our direction, we want slack water for an easy exit."

"Okay, have it your way, Skipper. I'll start breakfast while you shower; after we eat I'll shower. Rodger rolled out of bed. In one motion he was on his feet and wrapped Helen in his arms, "I'm pleased we can return to the ocean today and be real sailors again. But most of all, I'm happy you're on the mend, and back to your normal, sweet, loving, fascinating self."

"Hold it! Let's not get carried away, Mate," Helen countered. "Remember, I'm the Captain first, and your bunk-mate second."

"Not in my book," Rodger grinned happily. "Go get your shower and we'll finish this discussion later."

Helen grabbed her toiletries and disappeared up the companionway to the deck. While Rodger dressed, he mentally put together the ingredients for breakfast. *Let's see: eggs, bacon, hash browns, toast, juice and coffee. That ought to take the wrinkles out of our stomachs.* He lit the oil cook stove and set the coffee pot on to perk. Sticking his head out of the hatch he studied the sky. Cloud formations to the west, a feel of cool breeze on his face; should be a good day on the water. Turning back into the salon, he switched on the radio for the weather report.

The coffee finished perking. Rodger filled his mug to the brim. Putting two frying pans on the stovetop, he laced one with bacon, the other with hash browns. Placing the sour dough bread slices on a clean area of the stovetop for toasting, he decided to hold up on the eggs. Everything was nearly done when he heard Helen's approaching footsteps on the dock's floating walkway. Pushing the bacon aside he broke two eggs and dropped them into the same pan.

Helen paused on the steps of the companionway, "Oh my, that smells wonderful! Continuing into the salon, she stood on tiptoe and kissed Rodger's cheek. I've said it before and I'll say it again, you really are a keeper, Rodg."

"I'd like to think that my attributes go beyond my culinary skills."

"Take it from me, mate, they do. When God made you, she threw away the mold."

"She? Uh-huh. For right now I'll settle for the compliment intended."

After they'd finished breakfst Rodger headed for the shower. While Helen did the cleanup she listened to the weather report on the radio. The forcast was mixed, winds from the south at ten to twenty miles per hour with possible squalls. *We'll have the winds to move us even if they are hitting us on the nose, however we just may get wet in the process. Two-days should put us in Eureka where there's a well-equipped marina. Being two hundred nautical miles, that should be within our physical ability, and if all goes well, we'll be there in forty-eight hours.*

The Sea Witch rolled gently as Rodger stepped aboard, "Ahoy, Captain, permission to come aboard?"

"Permission granted," Helen called out, willingly entering into her part in this game of nautical etiquette. "My, don't you look shipshape in your clean blue denims, and matching ironed shirt, yet. You'll have to give me the name of your launderess."

"I must admit, I sent our things to the local laundry while you were convalescing. If you'll look in the forward hanging locker you'll find your laundry, clean and pressed."

Helen flung her arms in a spontaneous hug. "How thoughtful of you, love," she sighed. Their long embrace ended only after she playfully pushed him away. "Go topside and get the deck ready for departure, while I change into my freshly laundered clothes."

On deck, Rodger took the jib sail out of the sail bag, fastened it to the forestay, and then took the cover off the mainsail and the mizzen sail. Once the lines were in their proper places, all was ready for sailing. Starting the engine, he returned to the empty salon. "Ready when you are Skipper," he called out.

Helen emerged from the v-berth area dressed now in crisp, pressed, blue denims and shirt. . She pirouetted like a model, showing off her fresh wardrobe. "Thanks again for your thoughtfulness, Mate."

Rodger ran an appreciative eye over her trim figure, and then he sighed, "My pleasure, Skipper. I guess it's time we shoved off if you say slack tide starts in fifteen minutes. It'll take us that long to get to the bridge."

Taking her place at the helm, Helen eased the gearshift into reverse. The Sea Witch slowly backed out of the berth and into the waterway leading out of the marina into Yaquina Bay. Most of the fishing fleet had gone out several hours earlier and were either on their way to the fishing grounds, already fishing, hauling in crab pots, or reeling out long lines. The commercial boats were spread out across the water as far as the eye could see.

The magnificent arched bridge loomed high overhead, and a few tourists could be seen high up at the railing, watching the boats go out to the ocean and return. The outgoing river current, although countered to some extent by the incoming ocean waves, helped move the Sea Witch several knots faster than its engine speed. Rodger stood on the deck ready to raise the mainsail on command, the breeze ruffling his hair. Helen stood with the tiller directly behind her determining when the wind would be strong enough to let it take over. When satisfied, she called out, "Hoist the sails."

With Helen holding the bow directly into the wind Rodger grabbed the mainsail halyard and, hand-over-hand, raised the sail until the top of it reached the top of the mast. Cleating it off, he then raised the mizzen sail and jib. Caught by the head-on force of the wind, the sails luffed vigorously, like a dog shaking a rag. Helen let the Sea Witch fall off the wind, causing the sails to billow out to the port side. Taking the slack out of the mainsail, she checked the tell-tails; they were parallel to each other. Completing the task by winching down the boomvang, gave added downward pressure on the mainsail tightening it. Looking at the mainsail, she was satisfied that it was drawing wind well.

Rodger tended the jib and the mizzen sails in a similar manner. Cutting the engine, the soothing hum of the wind in the sails and the rhythmic lapping of the waves against the hull replaced the chugga-chugga-chugga sound of the engine.

They smiled at one another sharing the satisfaction of a job well done. "Hurrah!" shouted Helen to the winds, "we're sailing again."

Rodger stood and raised his arms skyward in a sign of victory.

"You know, Rodg, I think we have a good thing going here. High adventure, good companionship, good food, good weather, and a good ship beneath our feet."

"You're right, Skipper." He then settled back on the high side of the cockpit bench seat to be near Helen, yet out of the way. "What's the name of the mountain off to port, Skipper?"

"That's Mary's Peak according to the U.S. Coast Pilot book. It's about 4100 feet high and although the sides are covered with trees, the top isn't. I guess the timber line in this part of the world must peter out around 4000 ft."

The coastline became more rugged as they progressed farther south. Jagged promentaries and isolated off shore rock islands became the norm. Beaches were limited to coves and inlets. Only near the occasional sea town were houses evident.

"It's sure good to be on our journey to Tahiti again. It won't be so very long until we'll be looking at palm trees instead of fir, pine and cedar trees."

"Rodg, would you take the tiller?" Helen's voice suddenly grew thin. "I need to go below and lie down awhile. I don't have my sea legs yet, and I'm feeling woozy."

"You bet, Skipper. Rodger was on his feet and at Helen's side. I want you to always tell me when you need to rest, and I'll take the night watch. After you feel better, you can sail up until dark, and then relieve me at daybreak. During the day we can spell each other, as we need to. Rodger's eyes were dark with worry. Don't forget to take your medicine."

Once in the comfort of the salon Helen dutifully took her midday pills, then she stretched out on the divan. Watching the lamp's hypnotic swaying, like a hypnotist swinging a watch on a chain, she slowly drifted into sleep.

Her dreams were helter-skelter at first, but soon they included Rodger, the Sea Witch, and somehow the adventure that they were on. Except the adventure wasn't the sea voyage to Tahiti, but the adventure of their love affair. She saw herself standing, on a high rise of land bordering the sea, beside a stone cottage trimmed in white. Dressed in a frilly dress, not dungarees, she was running diwn a path towards Rodger, who seemed to be returning home at the end of a workday. Suddenly, above and behind him threatening storm clouds appeared to be bearing down upon him. They were about to consume him when she cried out a warning; she awakened to the sound of her own voice.

On deck, Rodger heard her cry out. "Are you all right?" he called down the companionway.

Huddled on the edge of the bed, her head in her hands, she fought to regain her composure. *The dream had started out so beautiful but ended so frightening. What could it mean?* She puzzled

Rodger scrambled down the steps to the salon. "What's wrong, Helen. My God, you look as if you've seen a ghost."

"Oh, Rodg, my dream. It was so beautiful in the beginning, yet became so frightening." Rodger sat down holding her in an embrace as she explained, "We lived in a cottage on a high bluff, overlooking the sea. I was running down a path to meet you; that's the good part. Then I saw this ominous black cloud forming behind you and moving like it would envelope you. That's when I cried out...to warn you. It was scary."

"Well, love, I appreciate your concern," Rodger soothed, "but all dream's don't come true. It probably just reflects your fear that the beautiful life we are experiencing right now could come to an end."

"Yes, I suppose you're right, but on the other hand, what if it's a forewarning of something?"

"Why don't you lie down again and see if you can continue your nap."

"Absolutely not! I've had enough of that dream. What's for lunch?" she demanded, determined to change the subject.

"How about a tuna fish sandwich, chips and coffee?" Rodger rose from the bed and moved toward the galley.

"Sounds good. Has the wind held while I slept?"

"Yes, we've been averaging 5 knots. A cloud layer has moved in overhead, but nothing to be concerned about."

"Good. If you'll fix lunch, Rodg, I'll take the watch. The Sea Witch can only sail herself, if there's nothing in the way."

"You and I know Genie really needs us: she can't chart her course, set her sails, or run her engine," replied Rodger trying to be light hearted to help Helen's mood.

"Okay Rodg," she laughed, "I'm convinced we're still in control, but how about that lunch, I'm starved. Genie can't do anything about that either."

✳   ✳   ✳   ✳

CHAPTER 22

▼

After lunch, Rodger slept while Helen scanned the water ahead watching for dead heads and other obstacles that might be a threat to their craft, at the same time she monitored Genie's readings. The weather remained overcast and the breeze held steady at fifteen knots out of the southwest. *This is a great day,* thought Helen. *It doesn't get any better than this. Rodger's tuberculosis is in remission, our relationship is wonderful, and the Sea Witch is handling beautifully.*

I'm able to function at about eighty percent of my former strength and endurance, so with the aide of our new electronics, we should be able reach our goal, Tahiti. Even if we have to buck heavy weather on the open ocean, working together, we should be able to handle, God forbid, even a knockdown because the hull is self-righting. While I appreciate Rodger's offer to stand a long night watch without a break, it's not necessary. Rodger has a health problem of his own.

The seduction of the steady lapping of the waves against the hull drew Helen into a deeper state of euphoria. *How I love that man and what a future we can have together, if only his tuberculosis remains in remission.* Suddenly a strong surge of wind in the sails startled Helen to full-attention. She gasped as the Sea Witch quickly heeled over an additional fifteen degrees, putting the rail in the water.

The sails need adjusting...now, her mind shouted. Quickly and expertly she let out the lines spilling wind from the sails. Soon the tell-tales were again parallel, and the list of the hull was less threatening. The sudden gust of wind had been violent enough to roll Rodger out of bed. He lay there momentarily trying to bring his thoughts in focus. *What's going on?* Groggily he slipped his feet into his deck shoes and struggled topside.

"What's up Skipper?"

"We've got a problem! A weather front hit us right on the nose. I guess I was daydreaming and didn't see it coming. Go below and get a weather report on the radio. We need to know what's going on up ahead of us and what to expect."

"Aye, aye, Captain," Rodger yelled over his shoulder as he ducked below deck. *Helen looks worried. This must be serious*, he thought. Hastily he turned the radio to the weather station. The report was out of Eureka, California this time instead of Vancouver, Canada. An offshore low-pressure area was moving rapidly up the coast around Point Arena the newscaster announced bringing 30 to 40 knot winds from the southwest. Scrambling back up the steps to the deck, Rodger relayed the information to Helen.

"This is a real blow," she shouted. "We'll turn into the wind to douse the jib and mizzen sail. But first go below and get the storm jib out of the sail locker."

"Aye, aye, Captain." Rodger did as instructed returning shortly with a smaller sail to take the place of the larger Genoa jib. Dropping the sail, he quickly unhooked the metal hanks from the forestay and replaced it with the storm jib. Raising it, he watched it luff violently as the Sea Witch continued to plow head-on into the wind and waves. Releashing the boomvang, he lowered the mainsail to be able to double-reef it. When hoisted again, it was a quarter of its former size.

Rodger dropped the mizzen sail, flaking and tying it securely to the mizzen boom. Helen let the Sea Witch's bow drop off to the wind allowing the storm jib and the reefed mainsail to fill with air. They now had forward motion and steerage.

"Good job Mate! Take the tiller, I'll go below and get our foul weather gear. There will be rain with this front coming at us." Changing places, Helen descended the five steps to the salon and then forward to the

V-berth area. Taking out the yellow slickers, bib overalls, sou'wester hats, and boots from a hanging locker she thought, *I've never experienced anything like this before; I hope I can handle it.* Donning her own gear quickly, she hurried topside.

Helen took over the tiller while Rodger hastily climbed into his foul weather gear and life jacket. "We've got to change course ten degrees to get more distance between us and the coastline. Be ready to tend the sails, as I swing the bow to starboard. The wind has been shifting from southwest to south, so we must be off Point Arena. After you trim the sails, Rodg, go below and dog down all the portholes. We'll put the hatch boards in the cabin opening when you get back. I wish we had harnesses; we would put them on and clip ourselves to a lifeline. That's something we'll have to get in Eureka for the next storm."

"Aye, aye, Captain. Anything else?"

"Yes, secure things below as best you can, then come back to the cockpit. We'll ride this out together. It might be a wild dance, Rodg, but I think we're ready for it."

Sounds of the wind in the rigging steadily increased, building into a crescendo known only to seamen under heavy weather conditions. The building waves, huge, turbulent, dark-green walls of water, rose above the Sea Witch. Like cruel sea monsters, they advanced upon the small craft and its occupants determined to swallow them up.

The bow of the Sea Witch climbed doggedly, steadily to the top of each wave, breaking through just before the peak, and then starting its slide down the backside into the trough, only to face another oncoming mountainous, wall of water. The strong wind blowing off the top edge of the waves produced a spray of white water and frothy foam; the spindrift, hurtling through the air like missiles, smashed against the dodger and anything in its way with a splat.

At the tiller, Helen, tense, determined, held the Sea Witch on its course. From the other side of the tiller, Rodger watched Helen intently as she commanded the boat to her bidding in defiance of the shrieking wind and the unrelenting waves. He knew his turn would come. He called above the wind, "Tell me when you want me to take over, Captain."

"Not yet! Let's hope it doesn't get any worse." She fought to keep the bow between fifteen and twenty degrees off the wind for steerage and forward movement. The wind wanted to push the Sea Witch broadside into a knockdown. It was important they keep steerage, which they had only if they kept moving forward into the wind and waves. Rodger continued to tend the jib and reefed main sheets by the winches, ready to immediately let up on them to spill air from the sails if need be. Failing to do so, the Sea Witch would heel over too far and take a knockdown.

"I've changed my mind," Helen suddenly shouted. "Take the tiller while I go below. I'm going to send a May Day message to the Coast Guard. This is getting worse by the minute."

"Aye, aye, Captain." Rodger quickly took Helen's place at the helm, standing as he firmly gripped the tiller. Helen ducked down in the protection of the dodger for a moment, turned, facing Rodger, silently mouthed, "I love you."

Rodger smiled and shouted, "I love you, too."

Removing the hatch boards from the cabin opening, Helen disappeared below deck. The wind howled like wild banshees in the rigging; the relentless, powerful waves continued to build higher. Rodger put the hatch boards back in place, making the cabin watertight. To keep from being thrown overboard, he sat down on the cockpit bench seat firmly holding the tiller with both hands as his adrenaline pumped. His senses heightened. He'd never know such exhileration. Throwing back his head, facing into the stinging spray, he shouted to the storm Gods, "Is this your best shot you sons-a-bitches?"

Holding the tiller, Rodger felt the sturdy strength of the Sea Witch through his arms and shoulders as she valiantly dove time and again into the waves. In his inner being, he had become an integral part of this gallant craft. Momentarily, he felt the ultimate power of being in total control…until he saw the huge, powerful wall of water coming at him, twice as high as the last, just as it crashed over them.

The Sea Witch shuddered from stem to stern. The bow, fighting its way out of the maelstrom, kept rising…too far…going over backwards. Turbulent, angry waters tore Rodger's hands from the tiller; he felt the stern fall beneath his feet. As his arms thrashed desperately to keep his head above the sucking, swirling water, the bow came crashing down on him. Mast and rigging, torn loose from the deck, hit him broadside taking him overboard…where he sank slowly and lifelessly into the ocean depths.

* * * *

Chapter 23

Helen sat, staring into the flames of the granite stone fireplace in her parent's living room. Her teenage niece and nephew, Joanie and Gregory, sat eagerly at her feet waiting for her to resume her story of the shipwreck she had endured two months earlier.

"Please, Aunt Helen, tell us what happened next? We know some of the story, but we want all of it," pleaded Gregory.

"You ask your questions, and I'll answer them the best I can," replied Helen without hesitation. "You know I had a concussion and was unconscious during the shipwreck." Helen sat back more relaxed now. "In fact, I was unconscious for several days."

"Yes, we know that," Joanie said, "but what caused the shipwreck?"

"A rogue wave hit us head on. The Sea Witch tried to climb the giant wall of water, but the wave was too tall and too powerful. I remember sitting at the ship's radio one minute, the next falling as the Sea Witch went over backwards. I felt myself flying across the salon; then all went black. When I awoke in the hospital, they told me I had been unconscious for two days."

Gregory, looking up into his aunt's eyes, then asked, "What happened to your Mate, Rodger?"

Helen, fighting now to control her emotions, replied, "Rodger was never found. The coast guard and others searched for days, but never located a trace of him. I'm told drowning is not such a bad way to leave this earth, but oh, how I miss him."

Joanie sat down in the chair beside Helen, extending her arm tenderly around her aunt. "What about the Sea Witch? What happened it?"

"Actually, she turned turtle. That's when a boat goes over backwards, then usually rights itself after a short time. This action took away her masts and swept her deck clean. Rodger had put the hatch boards in after I went below deck, this sealed the cabin and saved my life. The rocking motion of the waves and the heavy keel caused her to right herself. I was told the coast Guard found us soon after the storm, even though I hadn't had time to send a 'May Day' message."

"Where is the Sea Witch now?" asked Gregory as he continued to sit looking up at his aunt.

"Rodger had willed the Sea Witch to me. Since I decided to give up sailing for good, I discovered I couldn't bring myself to sell her. The Sea Witch is a part of Rodger that I can hold on to in a way. An old seaman, Rodger and I met in Westport, lives aboard her now at Coos Bay, Oregon. Aaron Bradley admired the boat and was in need of a home, so I invited him to live aboard and be its caretaker. He collects shells and paints the likeness of ships on them, like that shell over there on the fireplace mantel. That was a gift from him when we first met."

"Did he know about the shipwreck?" Joanie asked.

"No, not until I recovered from my injuries and drove to Westport. There he was at the base of the observation tower with his shells spread out for sale, just as we'd left him. He was delighted to move aboard a ship again, even without masts. The Sea Witch will probably never sail again, but she'll be home to an old sailor who appreciates her and loves her. When Aaron Bradley is gone, I may move aboard her myself. I thought about scuttling her, but changed my mind. She wouldn't be joining Rodger at the bottom of the ocean, he's not there. His spirit has gone on, and I pray that we'll meet again."

"What about Rodger's family?" continued Joanie.

"They grieve for Rodger, just as I do. They had a memorial service for him. I was invited, but chose not to attend."

"Why not, Aunt Helen? Why didn't you attend? I thought you loved him?" Gregory asked persistently.

Helen stood to emphasize what she was about to say. "I did love him, and I do love him; that's why I didn't attend; someday you'll understand. I had my own private memorial service for him. Rodger never made it to Tahiti, but he told me a few days before the shipwreck of a revelation he had.

He told me, 'If we never see Tahiti, this voyage has been far more than I'd ever hoped for. It's been a great adventure, but I've discovered, the greatest adventure of all is our love affair.'"

* * * *

CHAPTER 24
▼

Elbows on the bar, He studied the contents of his glass, then glanced again toward the woman sitting alone in the corner booth. He'd noticed her staring at him and wondered, was she someone he knew? He'd not gotten used to people staring at him, but at least he understood why. He was shocked anew each time he looked in the mirror and saw the angry red scar slashing upward from his cheekbone, across his temple, and then disappearing beneath the protective helmet his doctor had ordered him to wear. That might be why the woman was staring. And yet, there was something familiar about her, was she someone he'd known before the amnesia. Did she recognize him? He had to find out.

Slipping from the barstool, he made his way across the room, pausing in front of the auburn-haired woman in the corner booth. His eyes searched the woman's face, her grey-green eyes, then...the name slipped from his lips, "Helen?" It sounded almost like a plea. Startled, the woman's eyes widened, like a frightened deer about to bolt to safety, she sat riveted in her chair.

Confused, disoriented he turned on his heel and stumbled out the nearby door into the Monterey afternoon sunshine. Feeling suddenly ill, he leaned against the side of the building.

What had made me do such a foolhardy thing? he agonized. *What seemed so familiar about that woman? Why did I call her Helen...Helen?* He lifted his head, pushed himself away from the building. *Wait! Helen. Helen and*

Rodger. I remember...me...I'm Rodger...Rodger McCauley. But what am I doing here? I remember...a storm...something striking me on the head.

I need to sit down. Stumbling to a park bench, Rodger sank to its surface. *That's better. I have to remember. Before the storm...a sailboat...a wave, bigger than we could rise above, coming at us...Helen and me. Helen? Helen, my skipper, my lover...Oh my God...where is Helen? Is she alive? Below deck...I remember...she'd gone below deck...to radio an S.O.S..*

Rodger pressed his finger against his throbbing temples. *It's all so hazy. I know I live with other people at a place called Johnson House. I...I remember going there from the hospital. But how did I end up in the hospital? What was it they told me? Oh, yes. A fishing boat crew found me floating; face up, picked me out of the water, more dead than alive, about a mile off the Oregon coast, just south of Newport. With a cargo hold full of fish, they said they had not choice but to continue on to the port of their fish buyer. The amblulance attendants at Monterey insisting it was lucky I was wearing a life jacket.* Rodger's hands dropped to his lap. *Monterey! Why that's in California...hundreds of miles south of where we were when the storm hit us.*

Rodger stared out across the waters of the bay trying to organize the rush of sudden memories exploding like fireworks in his befuddled brain. *Amnesia, the doctor says I have amnesia. Tuberculosis, he'd mentioned I have tuberculosis that seems to be in remission. I think I need to get back to the Johnson house, get my head together to find out about Helen.* Rising stiffly to his feet, Rodger made his way along the familiar two blocks that had been his world until just a few minutes ago; Johnson House, the tavern, and the two-block walk between.

Nearing the two story white frame house, now his home, suddenly he stopped short. *I remember another house. A woman...Irene...people inside...my family.* His knees threatened to buckle; he staggered to the edge of the walk, clutching the boards of the picket fence bordering the carefully tended lawns. *Oh my God. My family. They must think I'm dead. And Helen—if she's alive. She thinks I'm dead too.*

Bill Smith, Johnson House's manager, sat at his desk sorting through the monthly bills when Rodger burst into the room. "Bill, Bill! I know who I am." Rodger leaned over the desk that separated him and Bill. "I know what happened to me. I remember the shipwreck. I need to find out about Helen. You've got to help me."

"Hallellulia! Of course I'll help you, but first calm down." Bill had risen from his seat and now guided Rodger to a chair. "Okay, John, let's start from the beginning, who are you?"

Rodger sank gratefully into the chair across from Bill. "Why did you call me John?"

"You've been John Doe to us for the past two months. We've been waiting for you to regain your memory and now, you have."

"I'm Rodger McCauley," Rodger began. "Helen and I were sailing to Tahiti. We ran head-on into a storm off the Oregon coast. Helen went below deck to radio for help. The waves were getting higher. I put the hatch boards in place after she went below to keep the water out of the cabin and keep her safe if we rolled over. Then a gigantic wave, too high to climb…water's in my face…a terrible pain in my head. I awoke in the hospital. Do you know anything about Helen? Did she survive the storm?"

"Well, first, glad to meet you, Rodger McCauley. Second, I'm sorry, I know nothing about this Helen. We would know nothing of the shipwreck here. Shipwrecks are common off the Oregon coast, but seldom make our newspapers. Is there any way you can reach your Helen? Do you know her phone number?"

"No, I don't." Then Rodger's face brightened. "But I know where she lives, if she's still alive."

"Great! We'll call information, they'll find it for you."

Bill dialed directory assistance, then handed the phone to Rodger. After Rodger gave the operator the address, it seemed an eternity before a crisp voice finally informed him, "Here's your number."

His hand, holding the phone grew moist, his finger shook as he dialed the number he'd scratched onto the note pad on Bill's desk. "I pray she's alive and I hope she doesn't have a heart attack when she hears my voice," he confessed to the manager. *What if she doesn't answer?* He agonized to himself.

"Want me to stick around?" Bill offered, then in response to Rodger's negative nod, waved a "good luck" salute and left the room.

The phone pressed to his ear, Rodger heard the click as the receiver was being lifted at the other end of the line.

"Hello?" a woman's voice...her voice.

Rodger swallowed the sudden lump in his throat. "Hello, Helen?"

"Yes."

"This is Rodger."

THE END

978-0-595-38488-4
0-595-38488-9

Printed in the United States
53575LVS00007BA/37-45